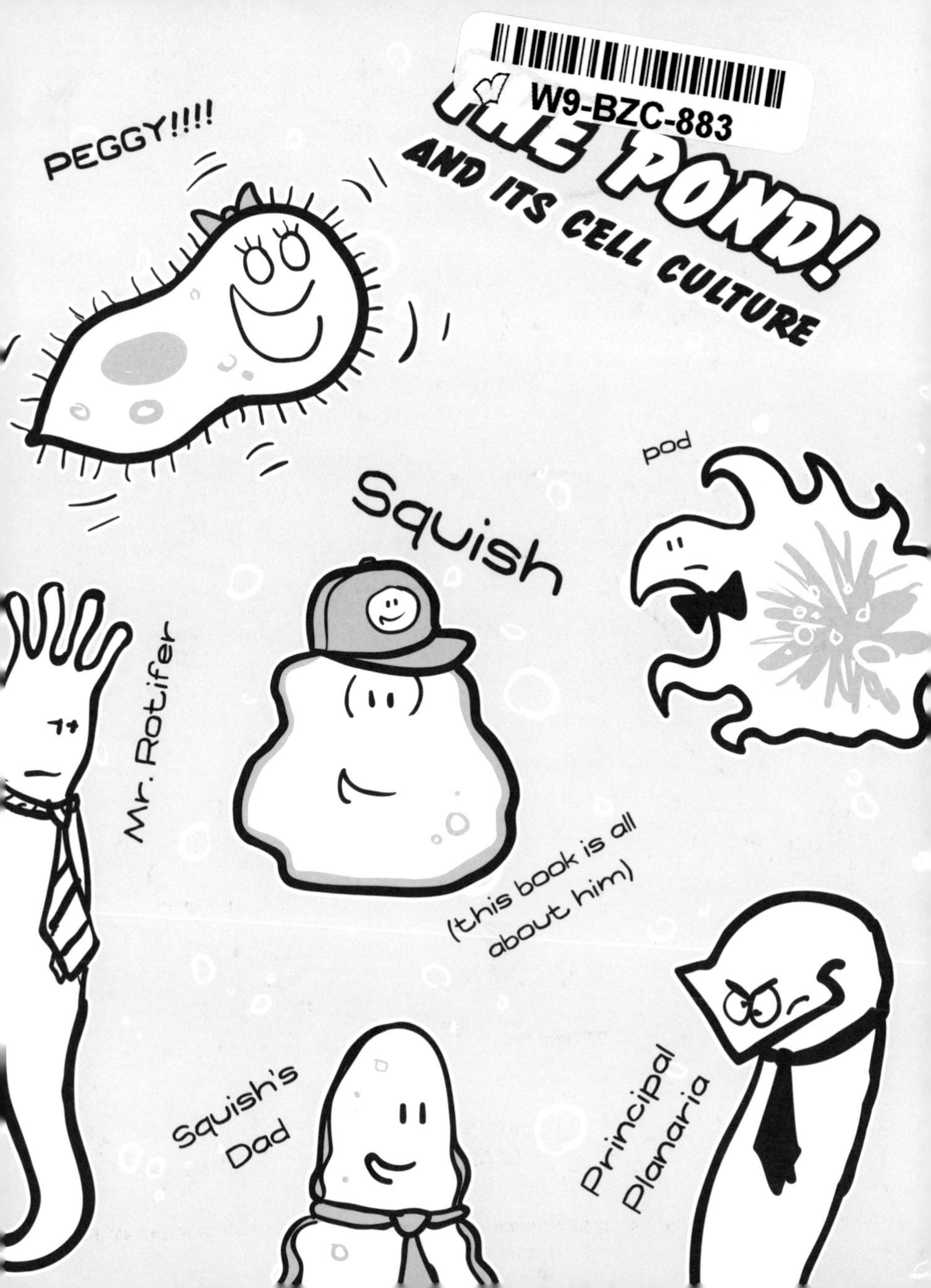
POND!
AND ITS CELL CULTURE
PEGGY!!!!
Squish
pod
Mr. Rotifer
(this book is all about him)
Squish's Dad
Principal Planaria

★"HILARIOUS. IF EVER A NEW SERIES DESERVED TO GO VIRAL, THIS ONE DOES."

—KIRKUS REVIEWS, STARRED

Read ALL the SQUISH books!

#1 SQUISH: Super Amoeba
#2 SQUISH: Brave New Pond
#3 SQUISH: The Power of the Parasite
#4 SQUISH: Captain Disaster
#5 SQUISH: Game On!
#6 SQUISH: Fear the Amoeba

squish
FEAR THE AMOEBA

BY JENNIFER L. HOLM & MATTHEW HOLM

RANDOM HOUSE 🏠 NEW YORK

Copyright © 2014 by Jennifer Holm and Matthew Holm

All rights reserved. Published in the United States by Random House Children's Books, a division of Random House LLC, a Penguin Random House Company, New York.

Random House and the colophon are registered trademarks of Random House LLC.

Visit us on the Web! randomhouse.com/kids

Educators and librarians, for a variety of teaching tools, visit us at RHTeachersLibrarians.com

Library of Congress Cataloging-in-Publication Data
Holm, Jennifer L.
Fear the amoeba / by Jennifer L. Holm and Matthew Holm. — First edition.
p. cm — (Squish ; 6)
Summary: Afraid to go to horror movies with his friend, Pod, Squish the amoeba feels better after learning that even comic book superheroes get scared sometimes.
ISBN 978-0-307-98302-2 (trade) —
ISBN 978-0-307-98303-9 (lib. bdg.) —
ISBN 978-0-307-98304-6 (ebook)
1. Graphic novels. [1. Graphic novels. 2. Amoeba—Fiction.
3. Fear—Fiction. 4. Horror films—Fiction.
5. Superheroes—Fiction. 6. Cartoons and comics—Fiction.]
I. Holm, Matthew. II. Title.
PZ7.7.H65Fe 2014   741.5'973—dc23   2013009098

MANUFACTURED IN MALAYSIA   10 9 8 7 6 5 4 3 2 1
First Edition

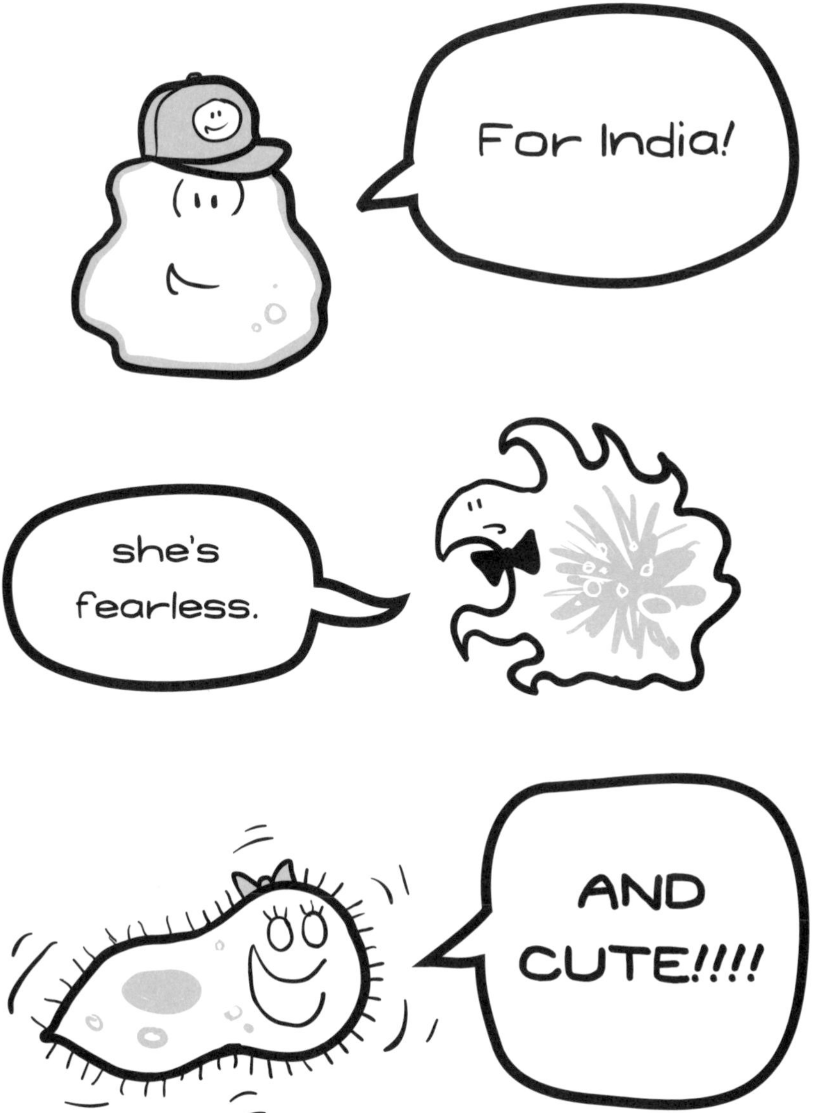
For India!
she's fearless.
AND CUTE!!!!

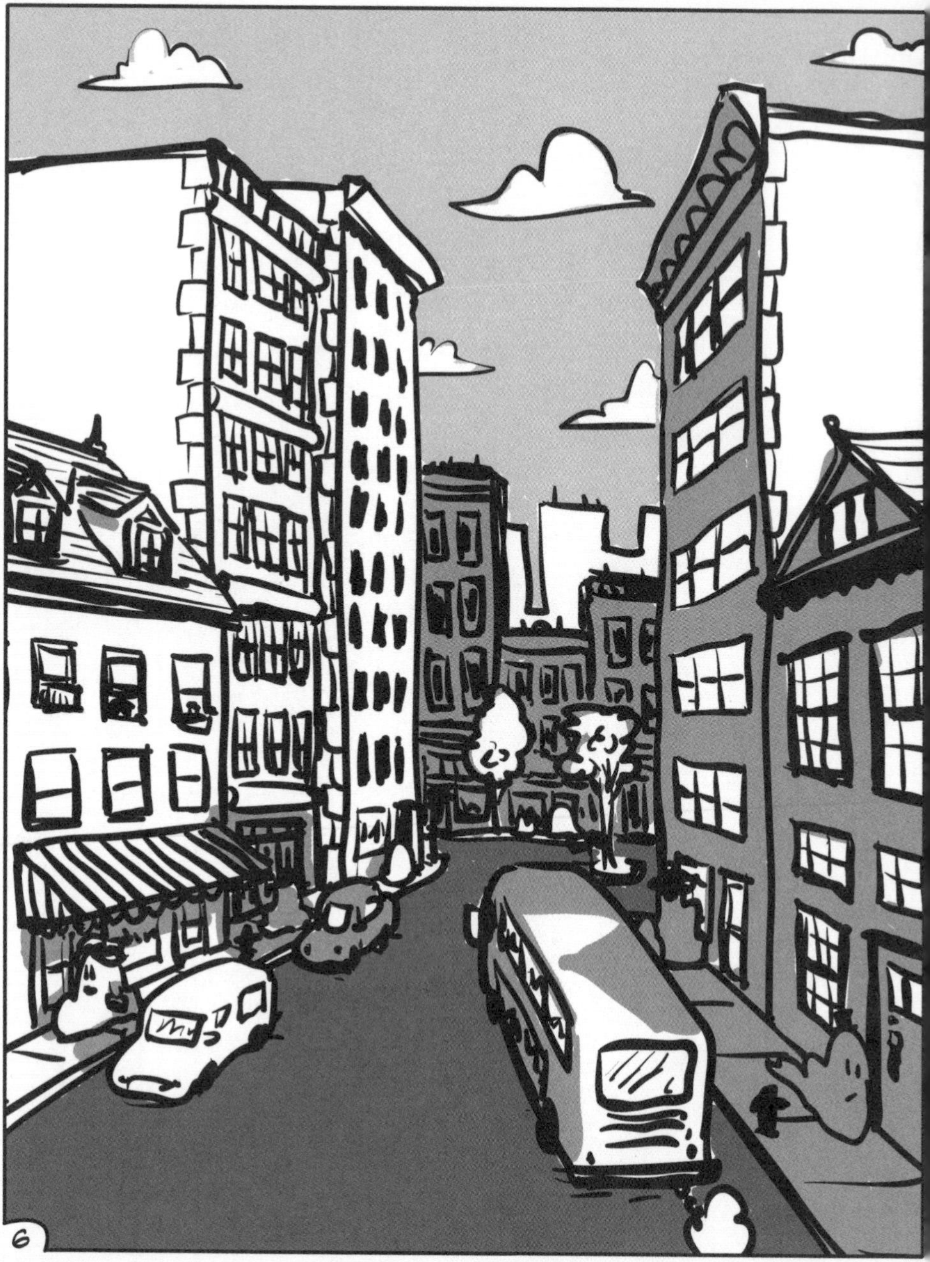

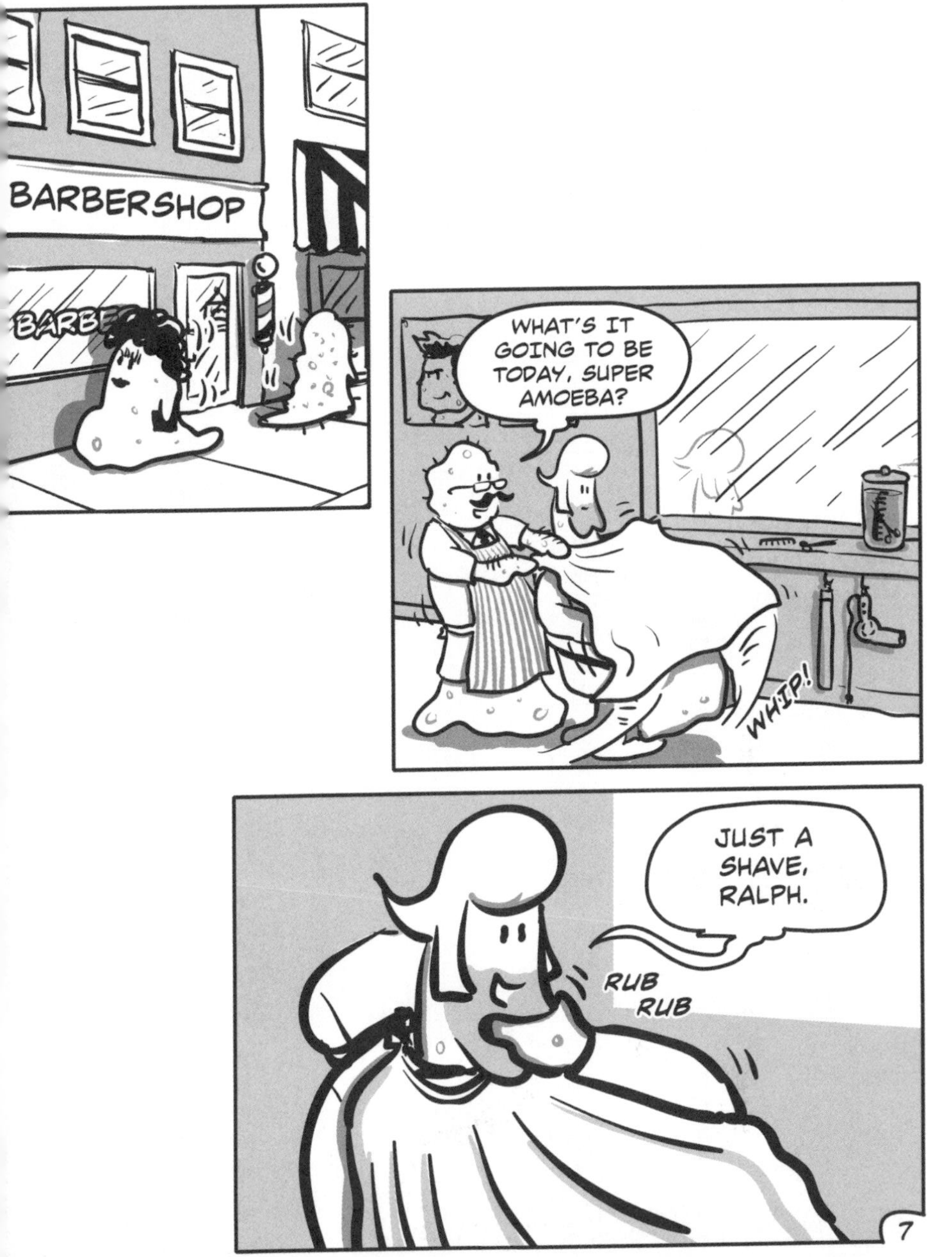
BARBERSHOP
WHAT'S IT GOING TO BE TODAY, SUPER AMOEBA?
WHIP!
JUST A SHAVE, RALPH.
RUB RUB

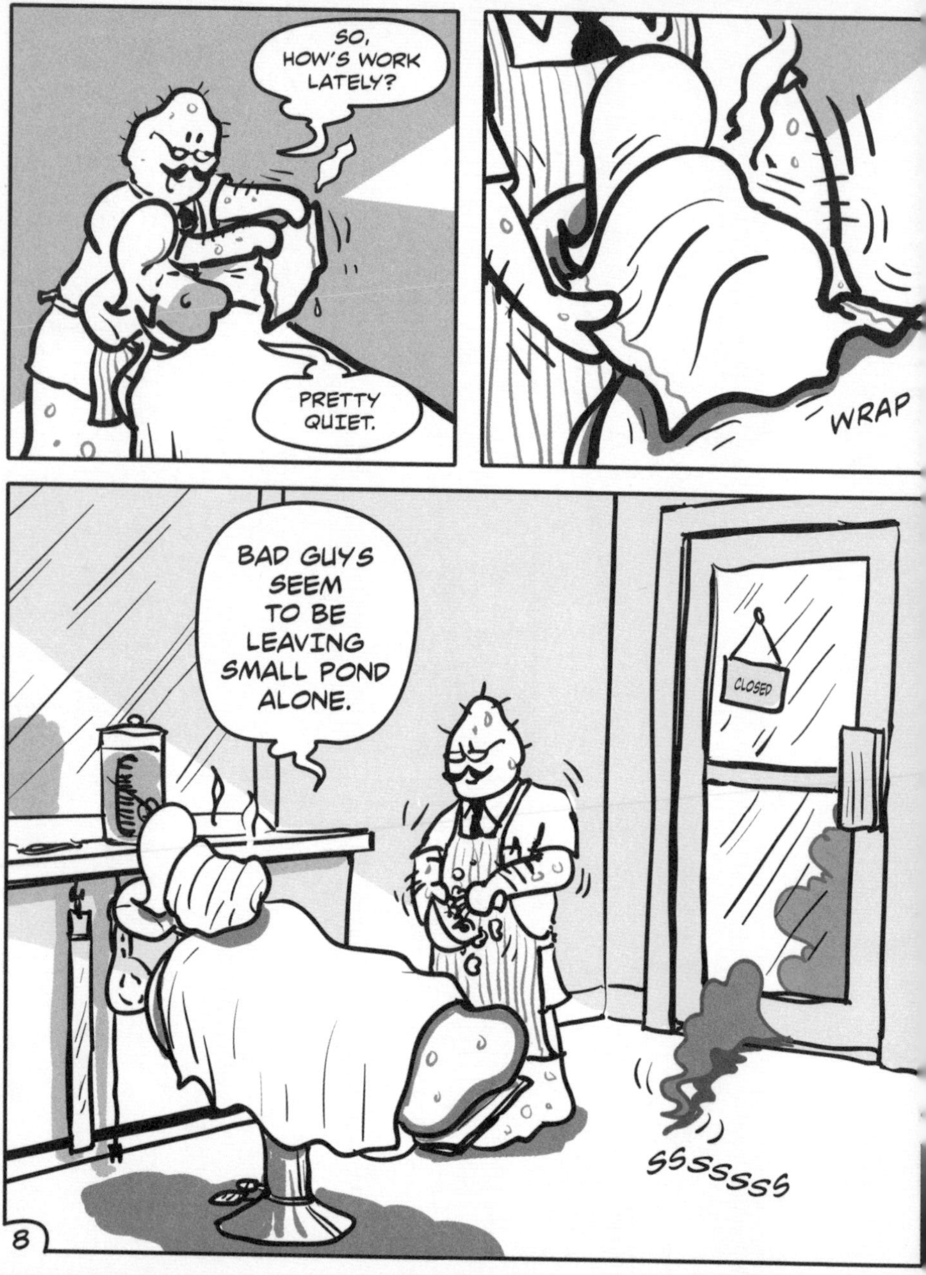
SO, HOW'S WORK LATELY?
PRETTY QUIET.
WRAP
BAD GUYS SEEM TO BE LEAVING SMALL POND ALONE.
CLOSED
SSSSSSS

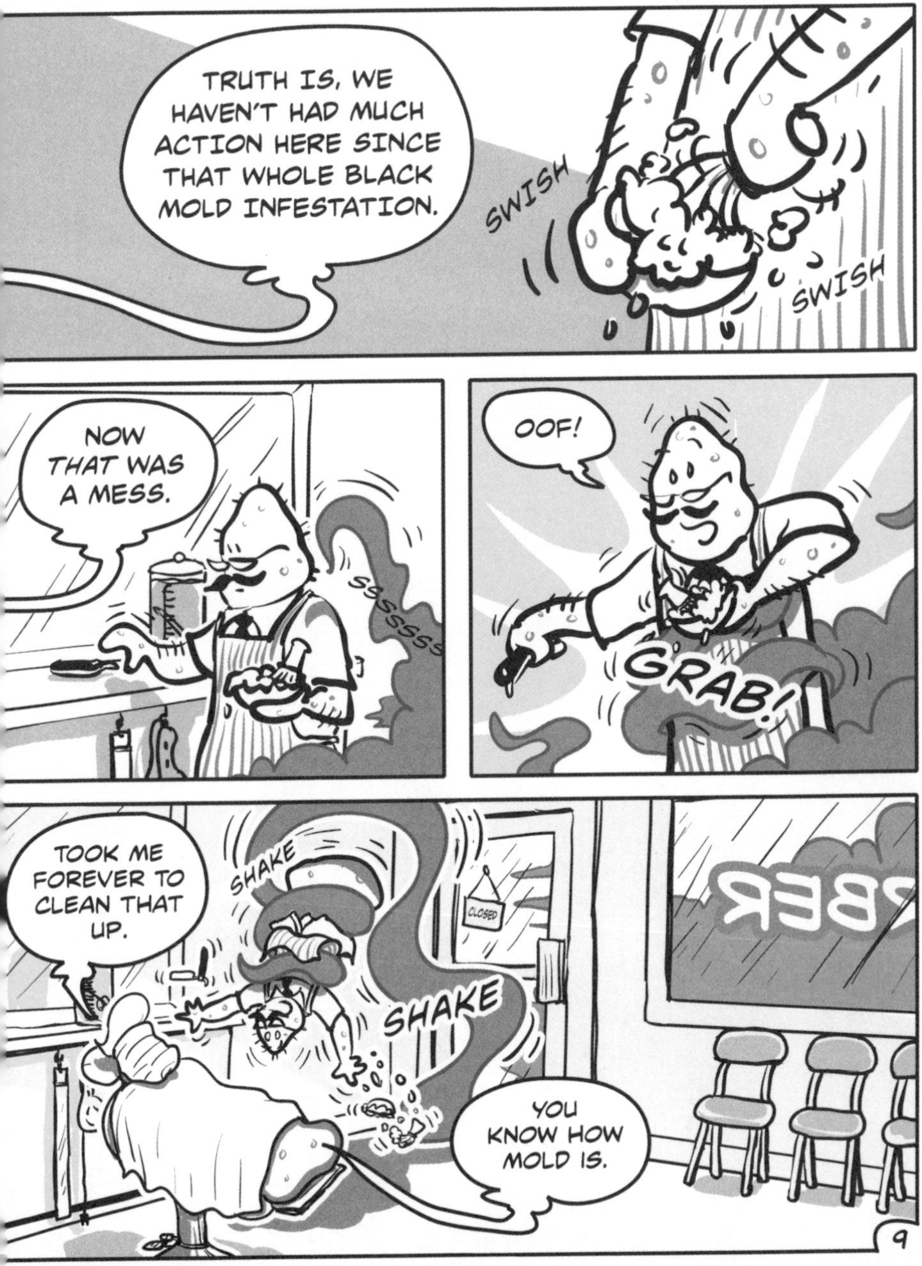
TRUTH IS, WE HAVEN'T HAD MUCH ACTION HERE SINCE THAT WHOLE BLACK MOLD INFESTATION.
SWISH
SWISH
NOW THAT WAS A MESS.
SSSSSSSS
OOF!
GRAB!
TOOK ME FOREVER TO CLEAN THAT UP.
SHAKE
CLOSED
SHAKE
YOU KNOW HOW MOLD IS.

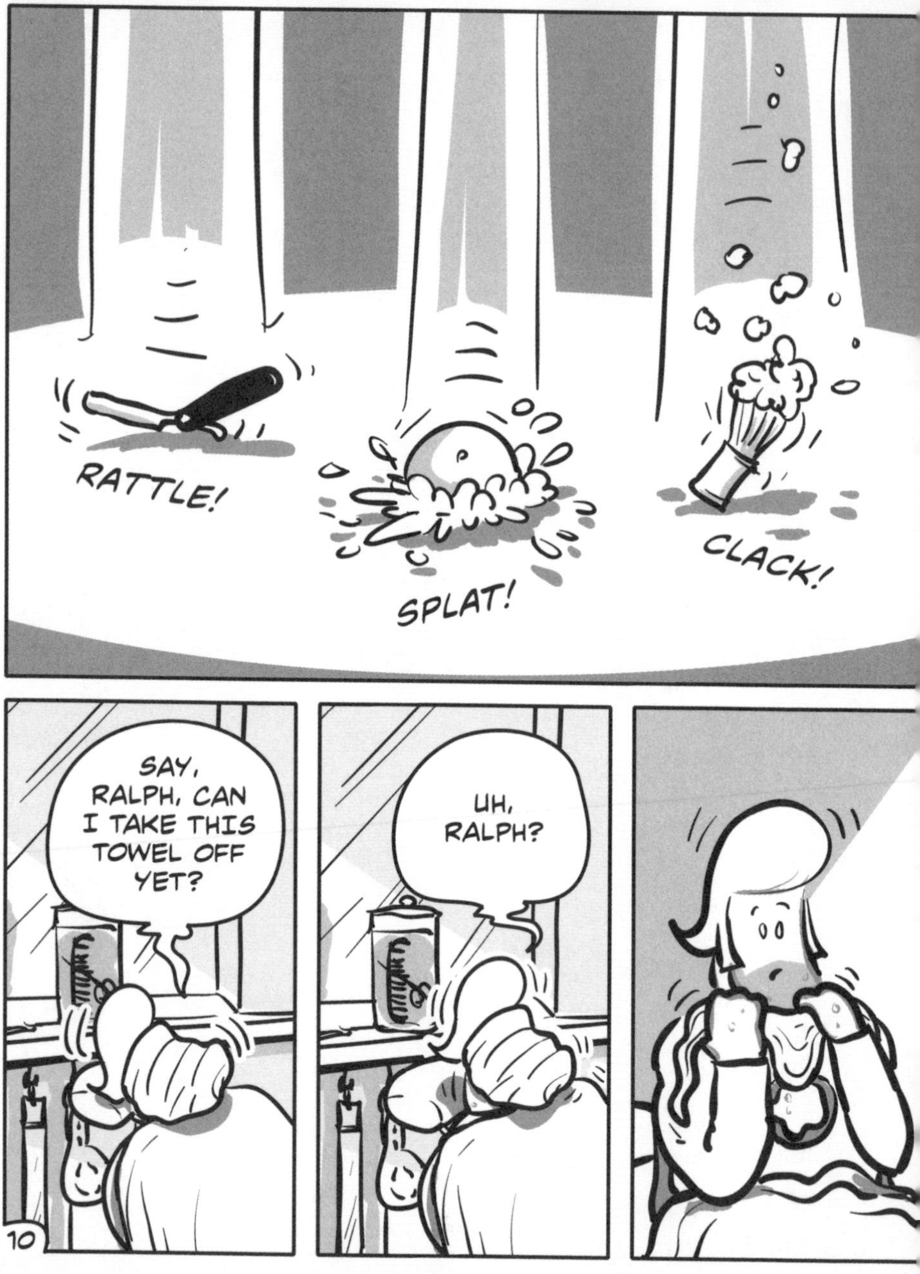
RATTLE!
SPLAT!
CLACK!
SAY, RALPH, CAN I TAKE THIS TOWEL OFF YET?
UH, RALPH?

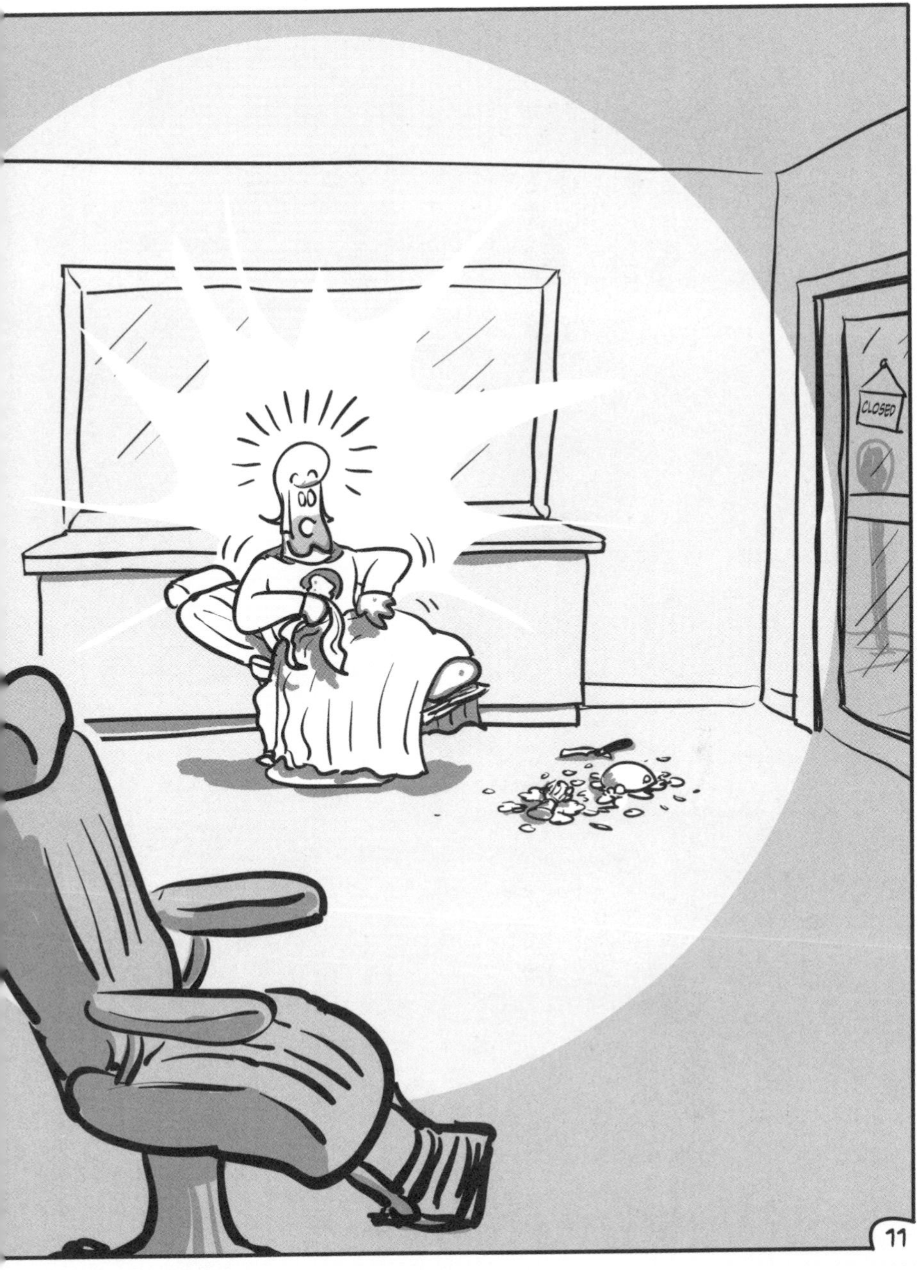
CLOSED

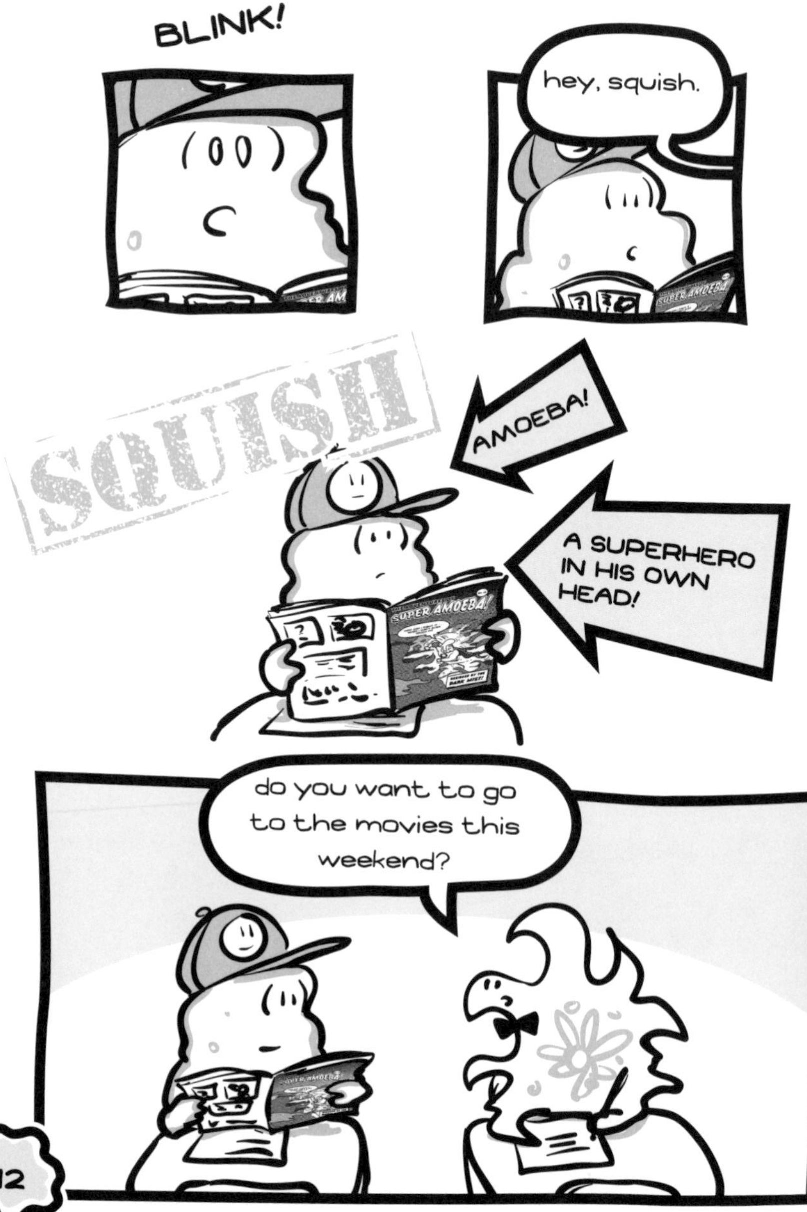
BLINK!
hey, squish.
SQUISH
AMOEBA!
A SUPERHERO IN HIS OWN HEAD!
do you want to go to the movies this weekend?

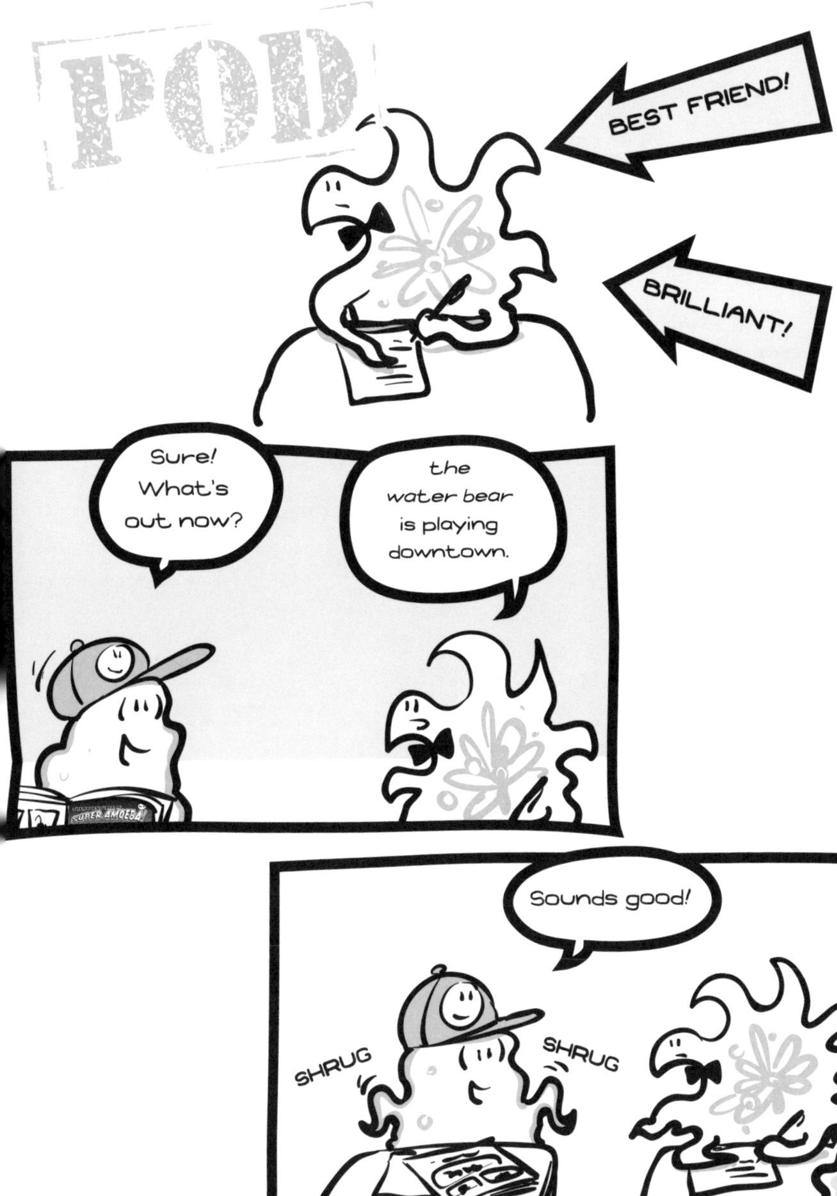
POD
BEST FRIEND!
BRILLIANT!
Sure! What's out now?
the water bear is playing downtown.
SUPER AMOEBA!
Sounds good!
SHRUG
SHRUG

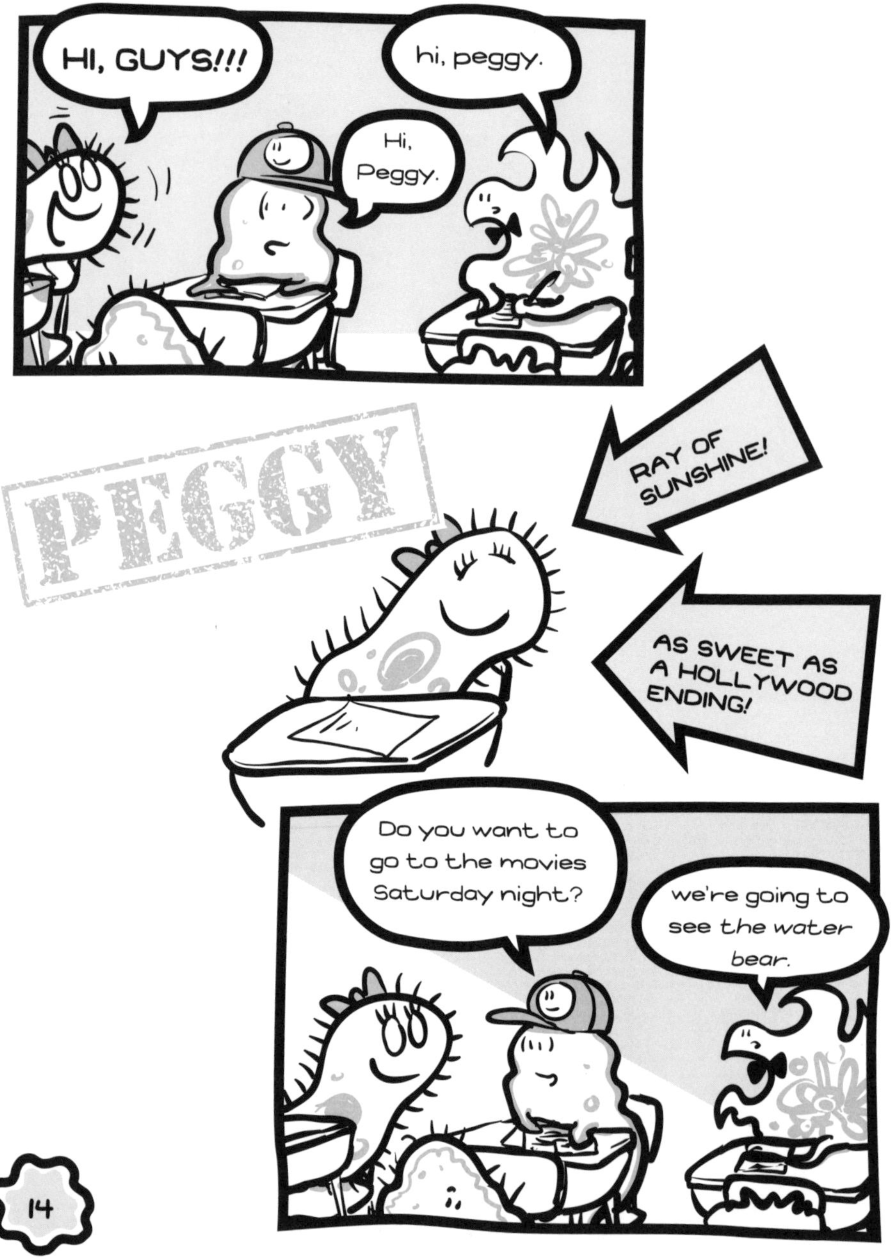
HI, GUYS!!!
hi, peggy.
Hi, Peggy.
PEGGY
RAY OF SUNSHINE!
AS SWEET AS A HOLLYWOOD ENDING!
Do you want to go to the movies Saturday night?
we're going to see the water bear.

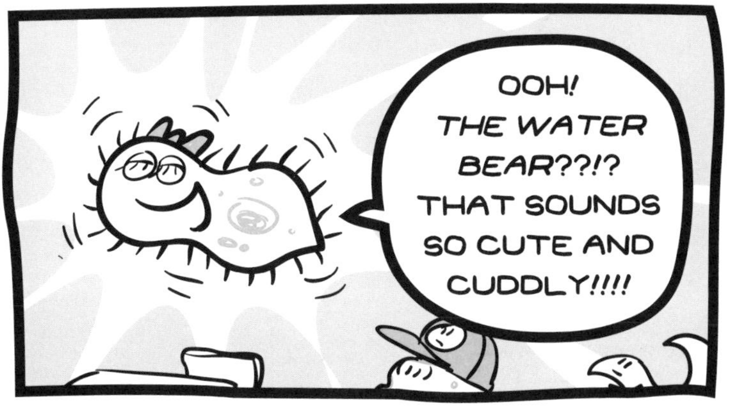
OOH!
THE WATER BEAR??!? THAT SOUNDS SO CUTE AND CUDDLY!!!!

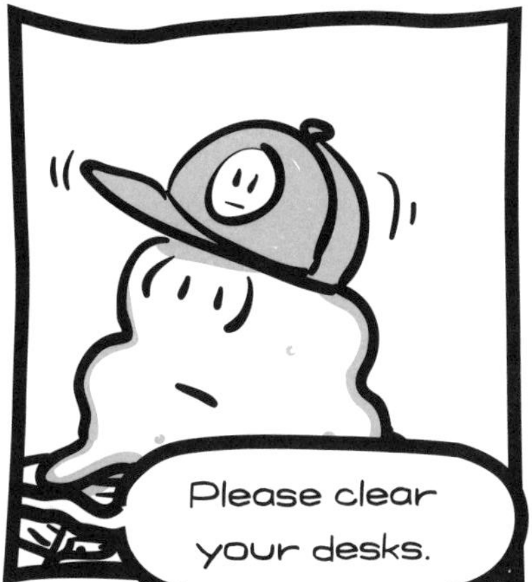
Please clear your desks.

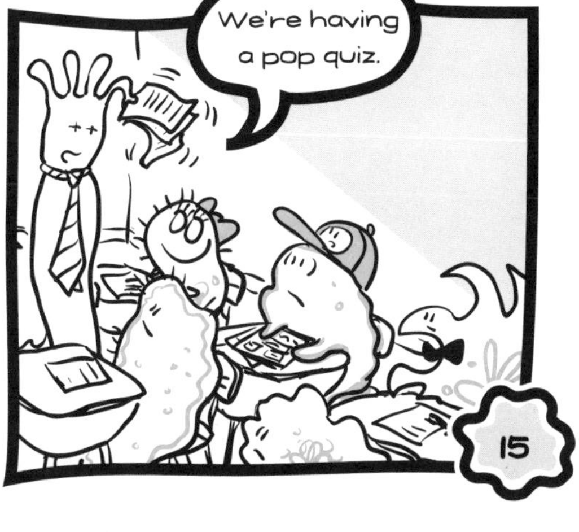
We're having a pop quiz.

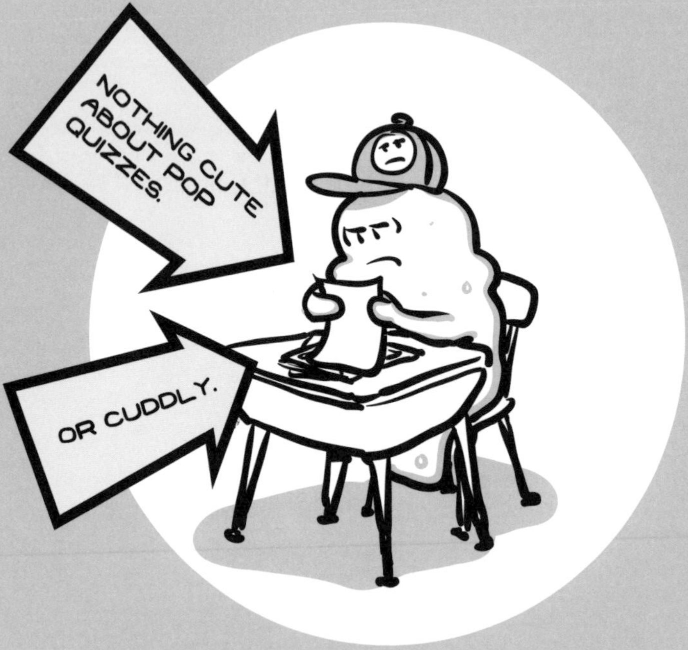
NOTHING CUTE ABOUT POP QUIZZES.
OR CUDDLY.

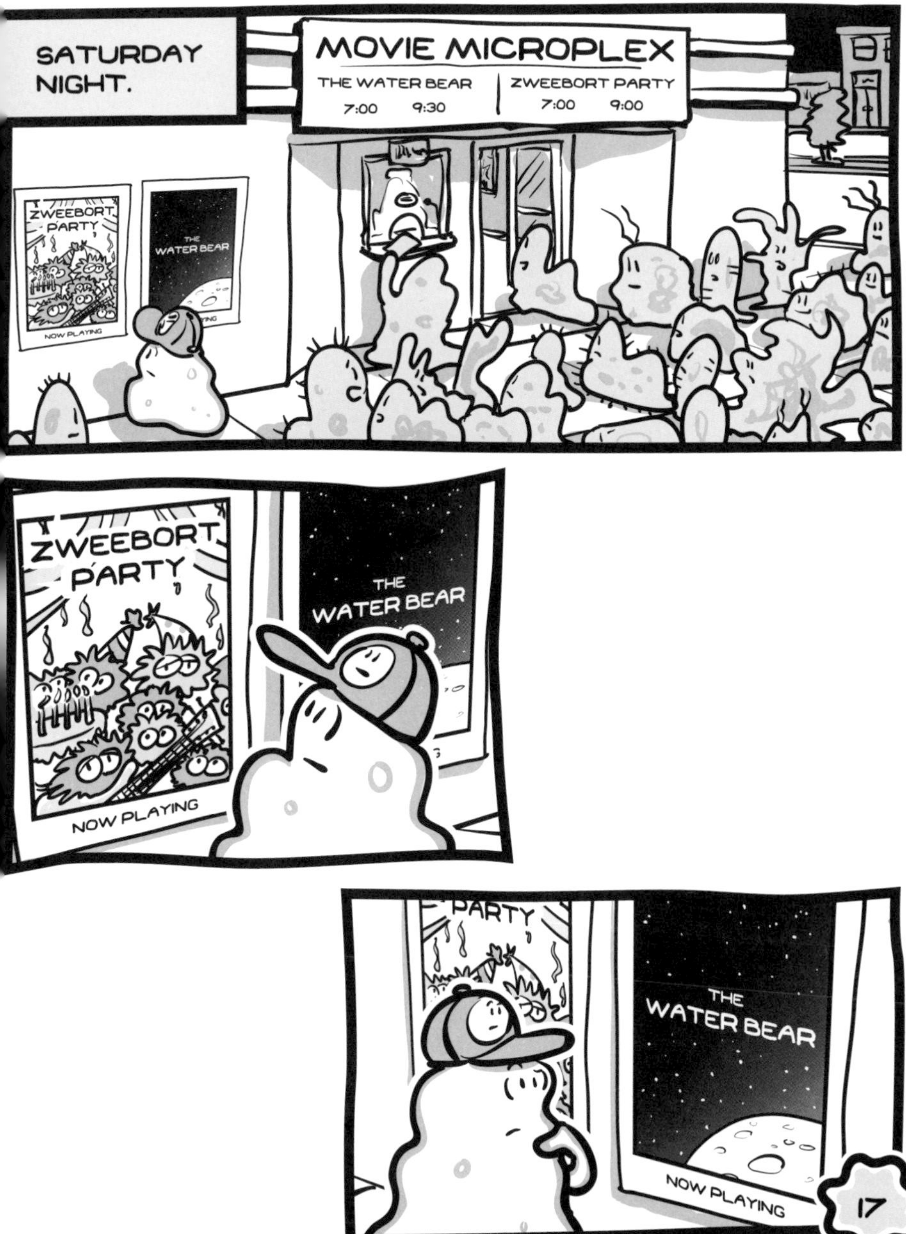
SATURDAY NIGHT.
MOVIE MICROPLEX
THE WATER BEAR 7:00 9:30
ZWEEBORT PARTY 7:00 9:00
ZWEEBORT PARTY
THE WATER BEAR
NOW PLAYING
ZWEEBORT PARTY
NOW PLAYING
THE WATER BEAR
PARTY
THE WATER BEAR
NOW PLAYING

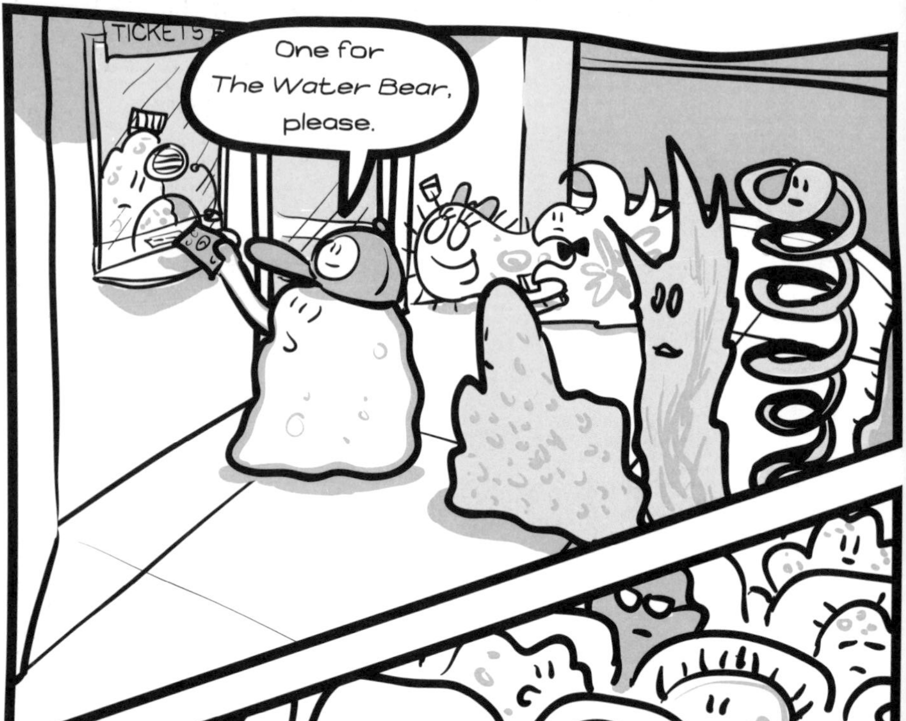
TICKETS
One for The Water Bear, please.

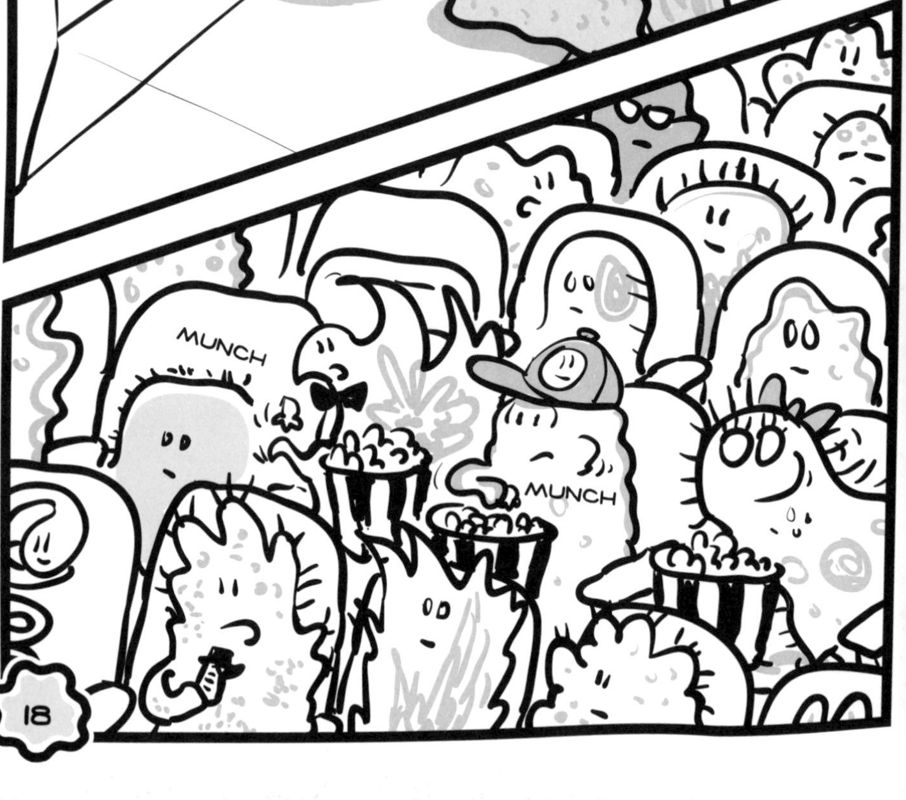
MUNCH
MUNCH

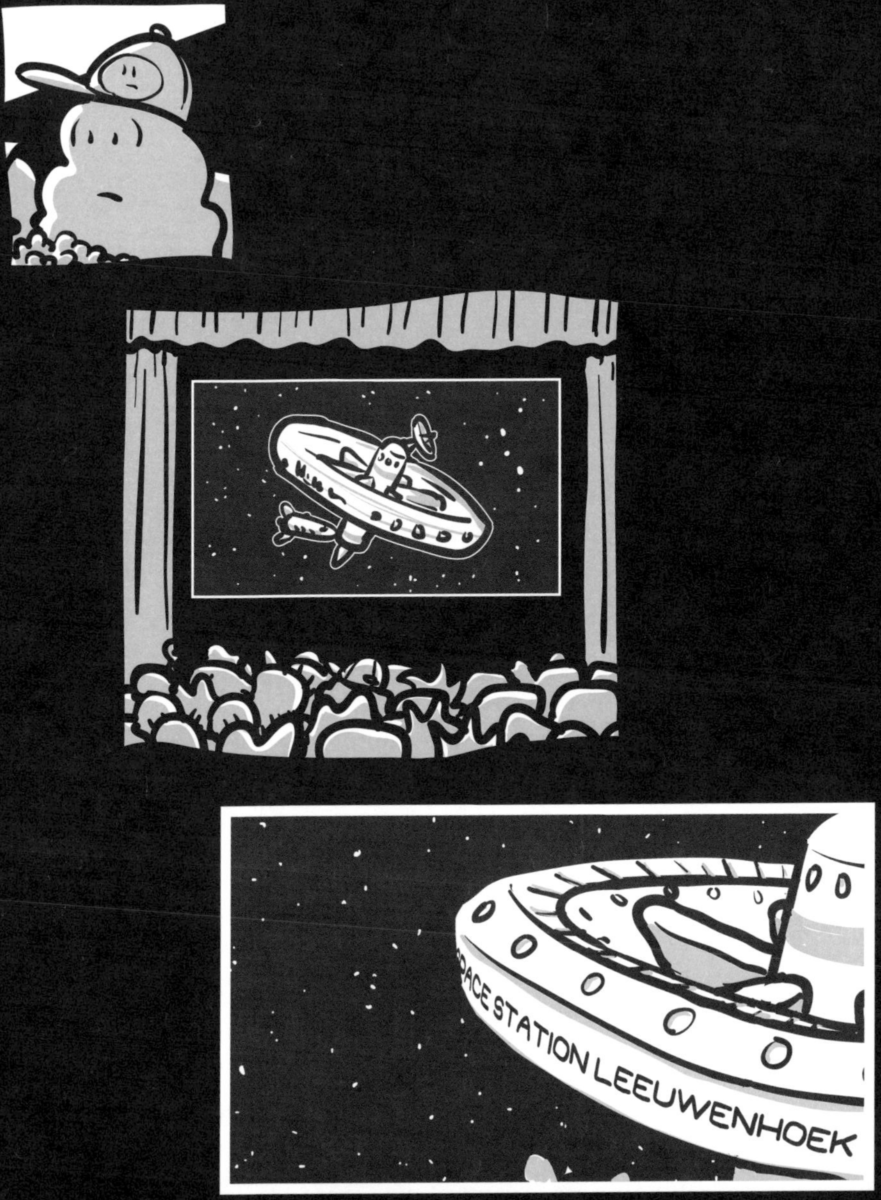
PACE STATION LEEUWENHOEK

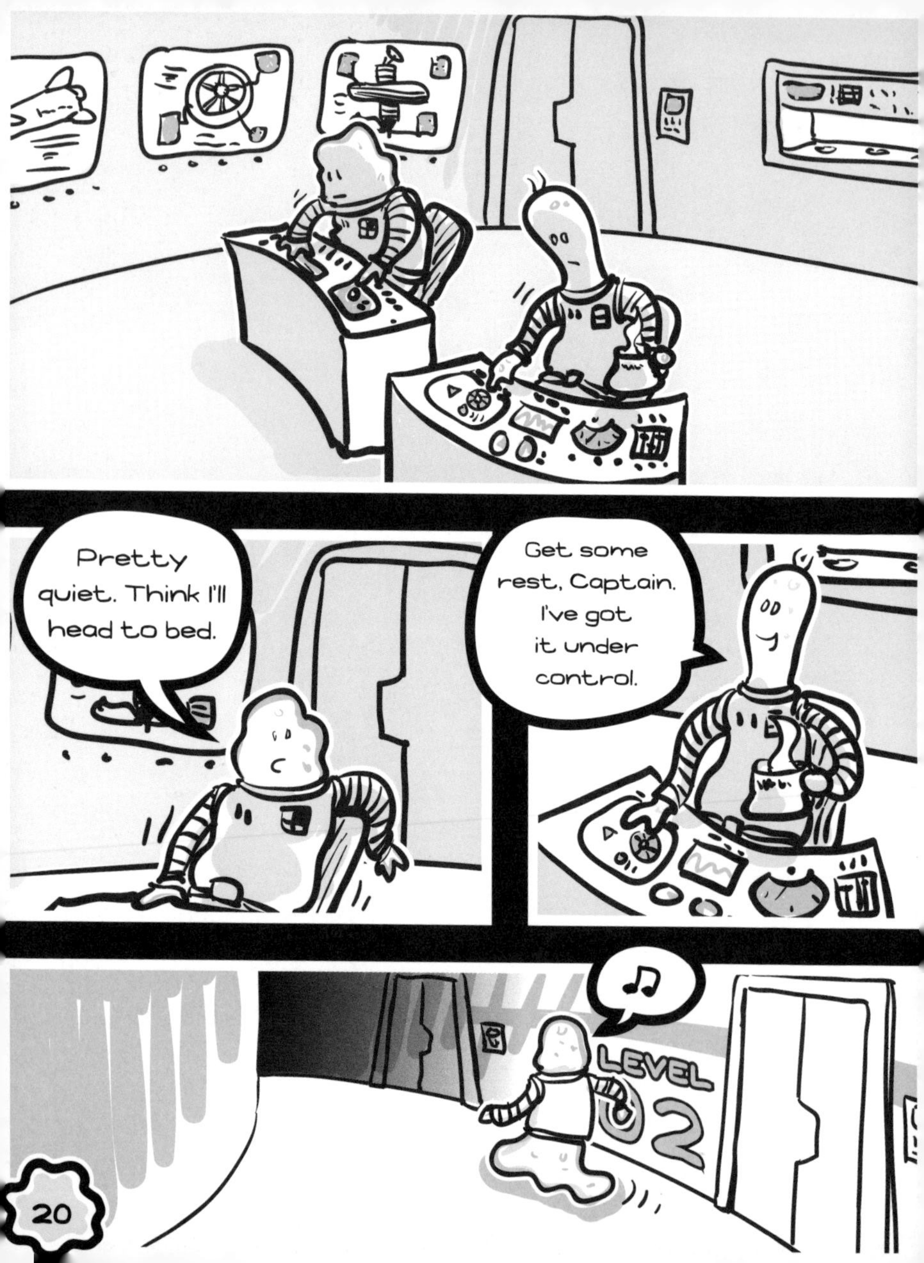
Pretty quiet. Think I'll head to bed.
Get some rest, Captain. I've got it under control.
LEVEL 02

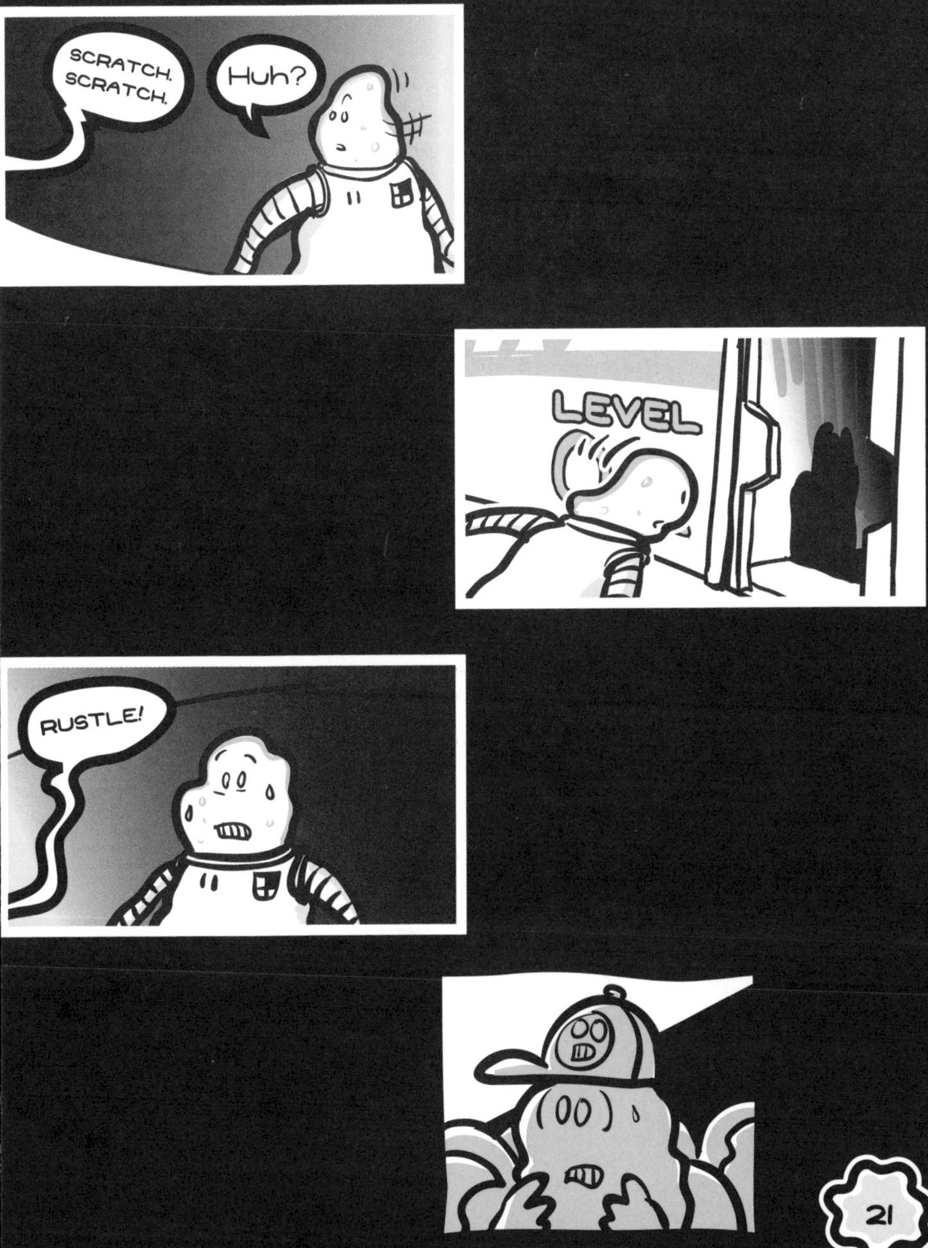
SCRATCH. SCRATCH.
Huh?
LEVEL
RUSTLE!

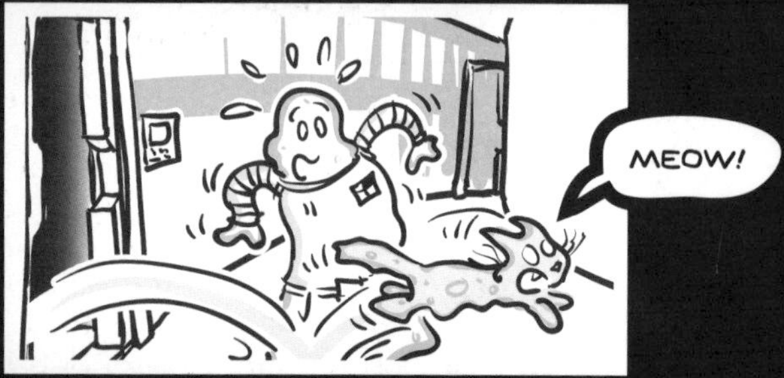
MEOW!

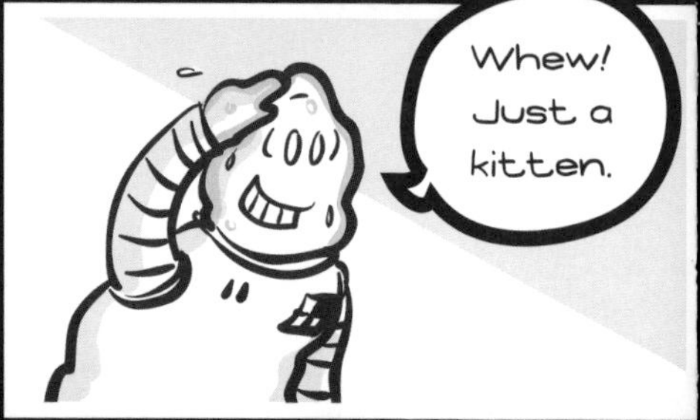
Whew! Just a kitten.

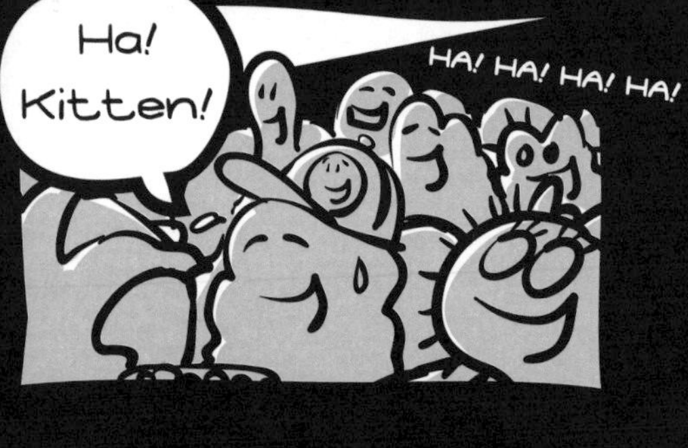
Ha! Kitten!
HA! HA! HA! HA!

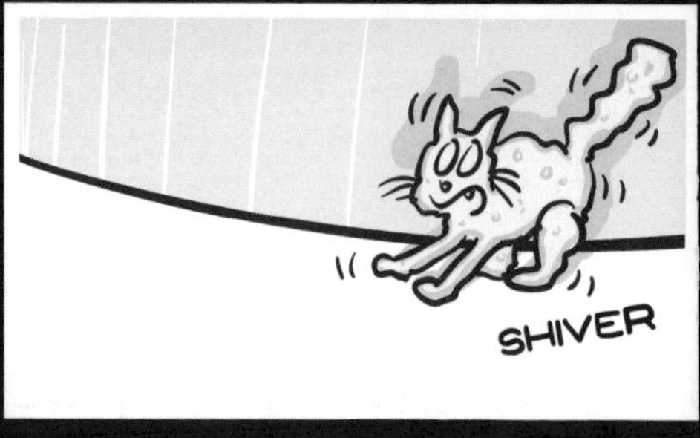
SHIVER

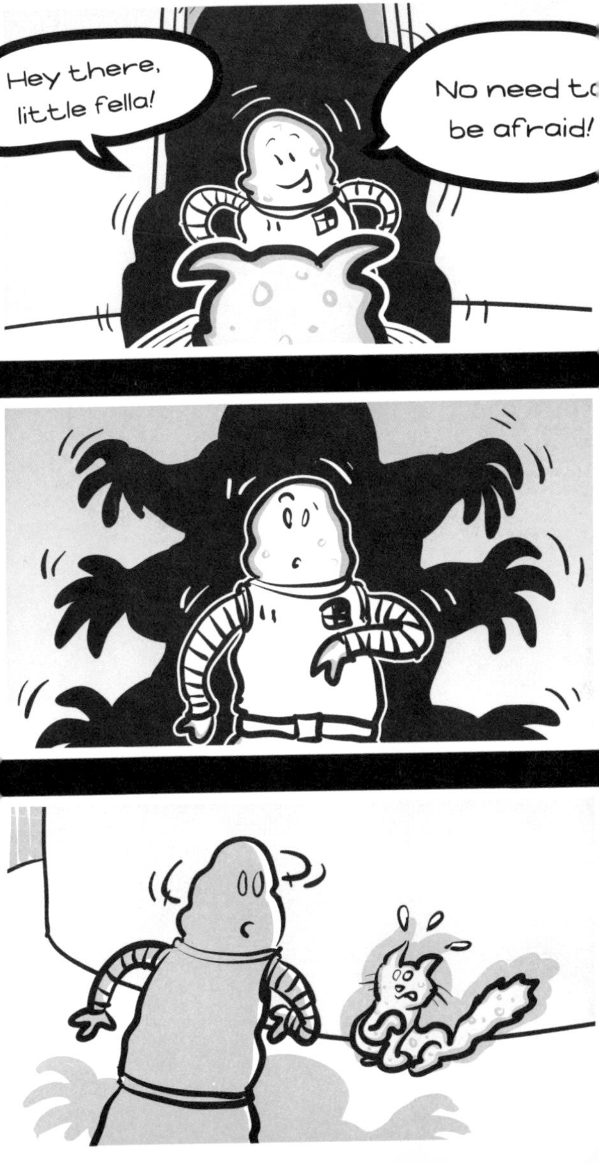
Hey there, little fella!
No need to be afraid!

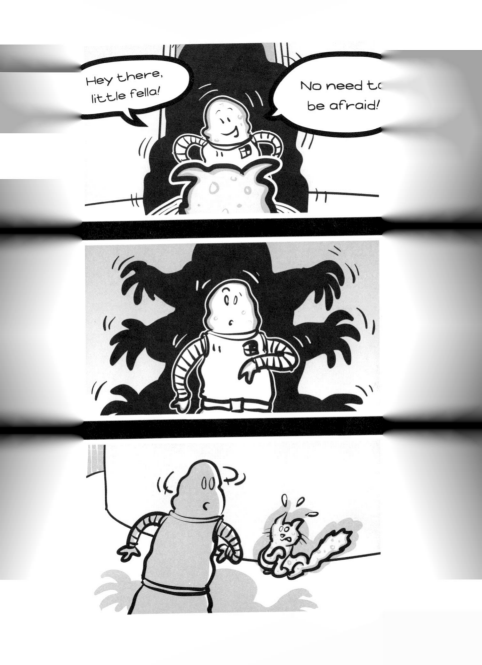

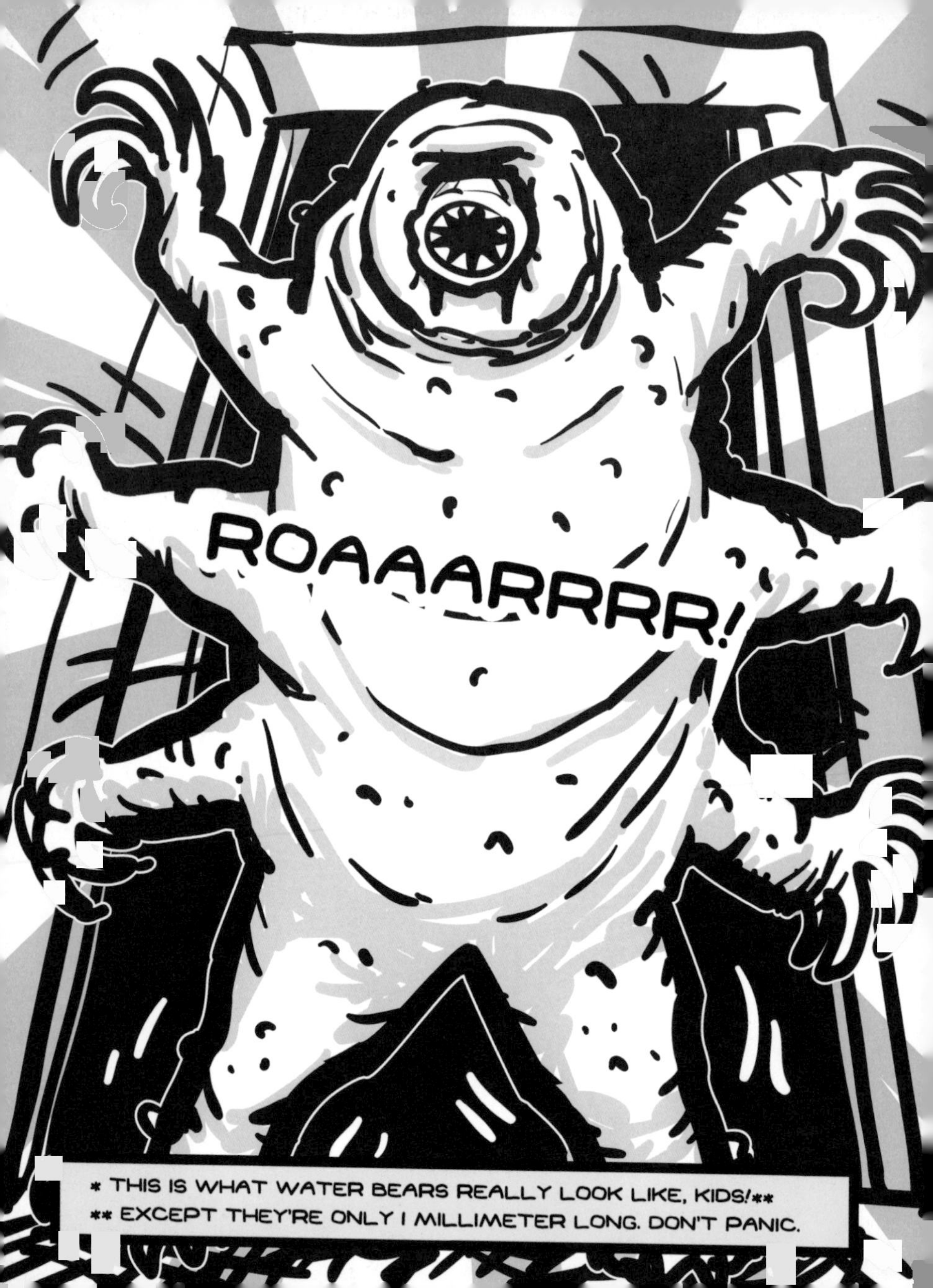
ROAAAARRRRR!
* THIS IS WHAT WATER BEARS REALLY LOOK LIKE, KIDS!**
** EXCEPT THEY'RE ONLY 1 MILLIMETER LONG. DON'T PANIC.

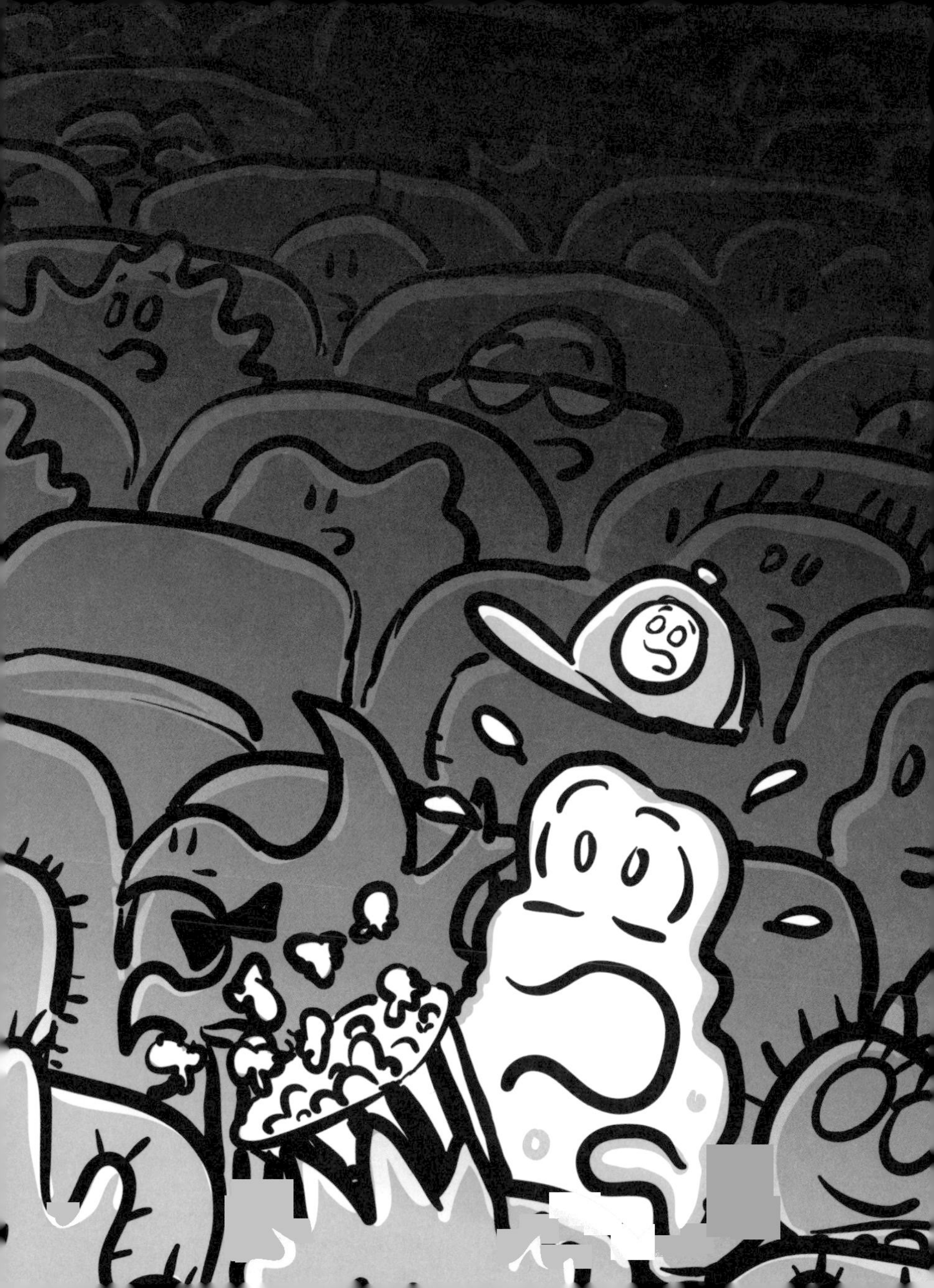

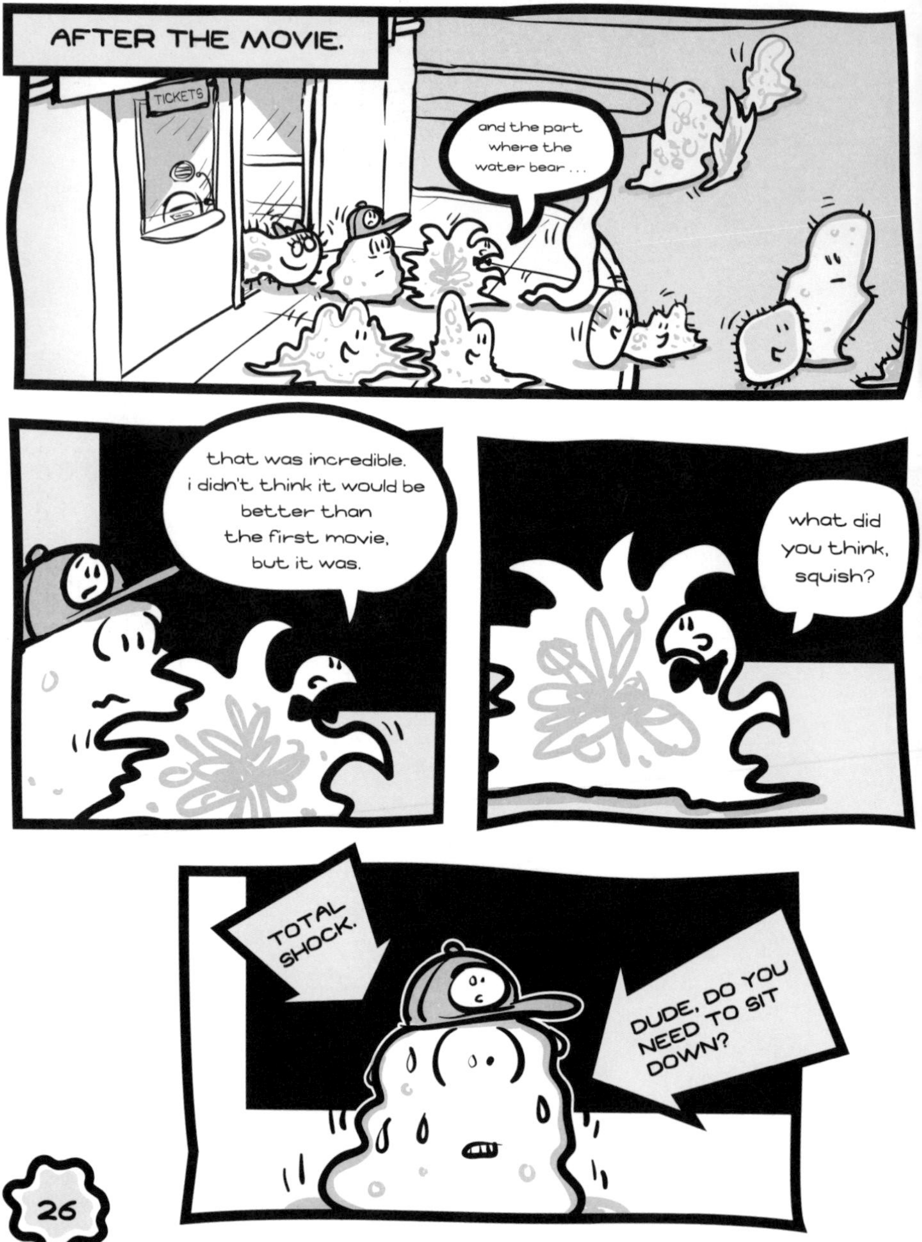
AFTER THE MOVIE.
TICKETS
and the part where the water bear . . .
that was incredible. i didn't think it would be better than the first movie, but it was.
what did you think, squish?
TOTAL SHOCK.
DUDE, DO YOU NEED TO SIT DOWN?

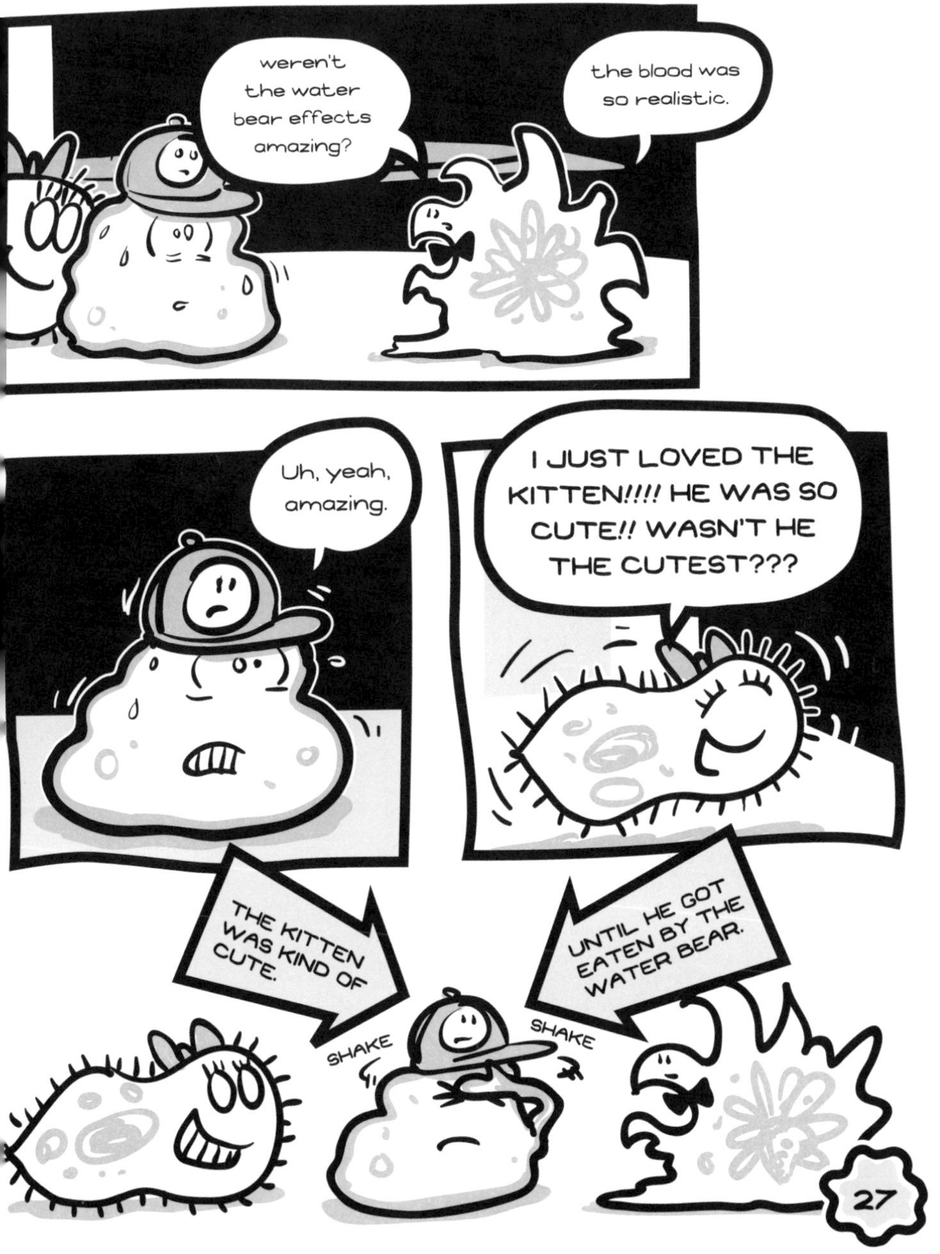
weren't the water bear effects amazing?
the blood was so realistic.
Uh, yeah, amazing.
I JUST LOVED THE KITTEN!!!!! HE WAS SO CUTE!! WASN'T HE THE CUTEST???
THE KITTEN WAS KIND OF CUTE.
UNTIL HE GOT EATEN BY THE WATER BEAR.
SHAKE
SHAKE

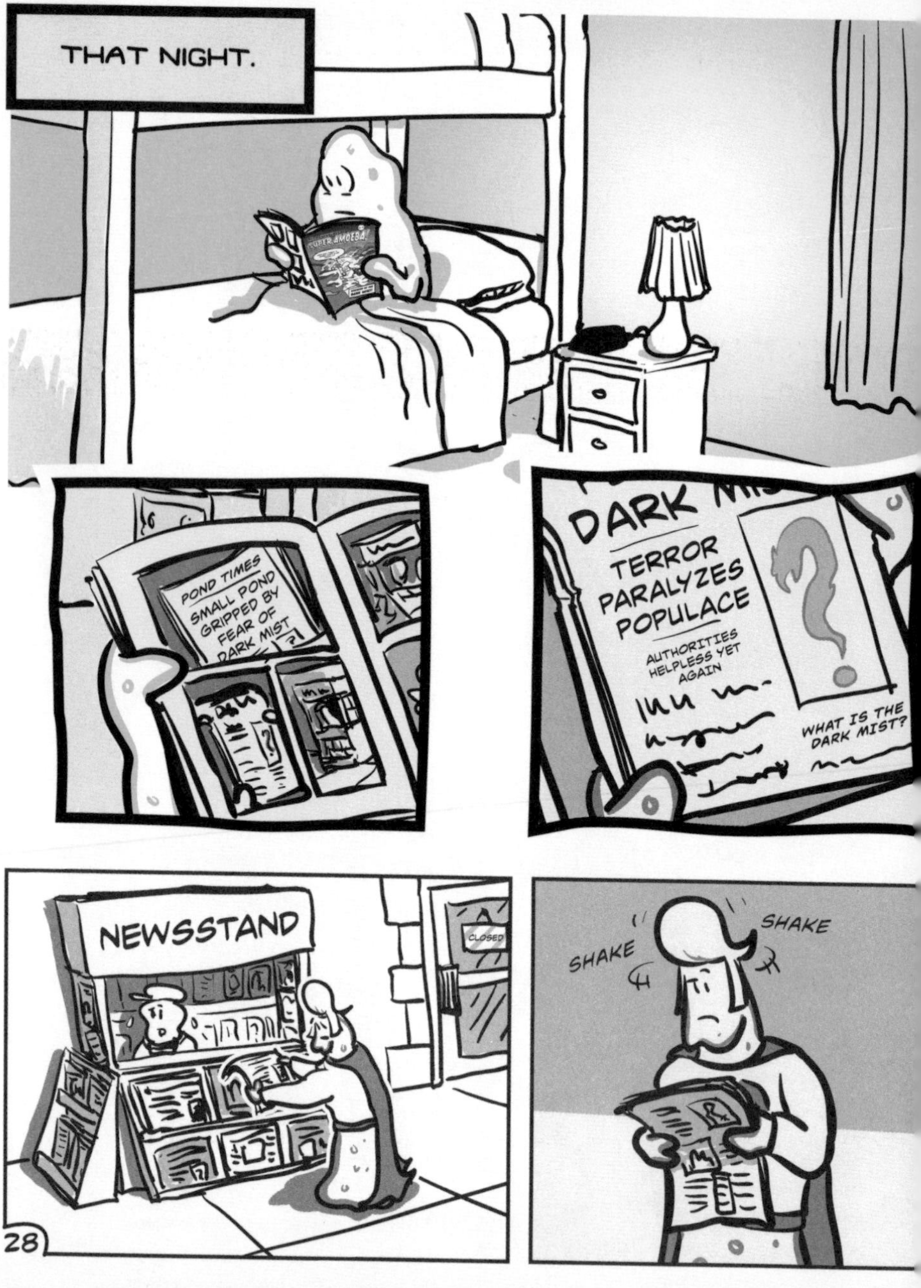
THAT NIGHT.
SUPER AMOEBA!
POND TIMES
SMALL POND GRIPPED BY FEAR OF DARK MIST
DARK
TERROR PARALYZES POPULACE
AUTHORITIES HELPLESS YET AGAIN
WHAT IS THE DARK MIST?
NEWSSTAND
CLOSED
SHAKE
SHAKE

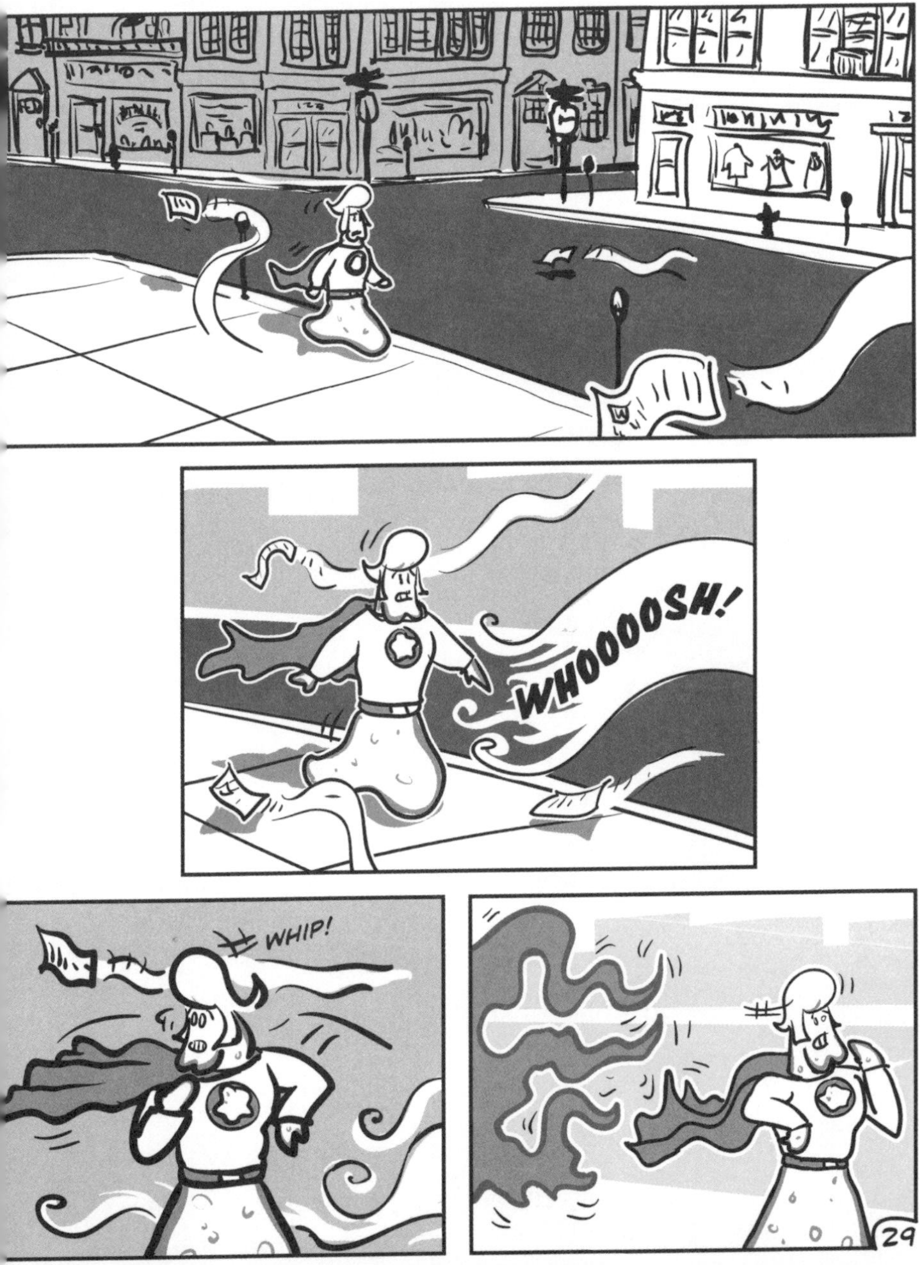
WHOOOOOSH!
WHIP!

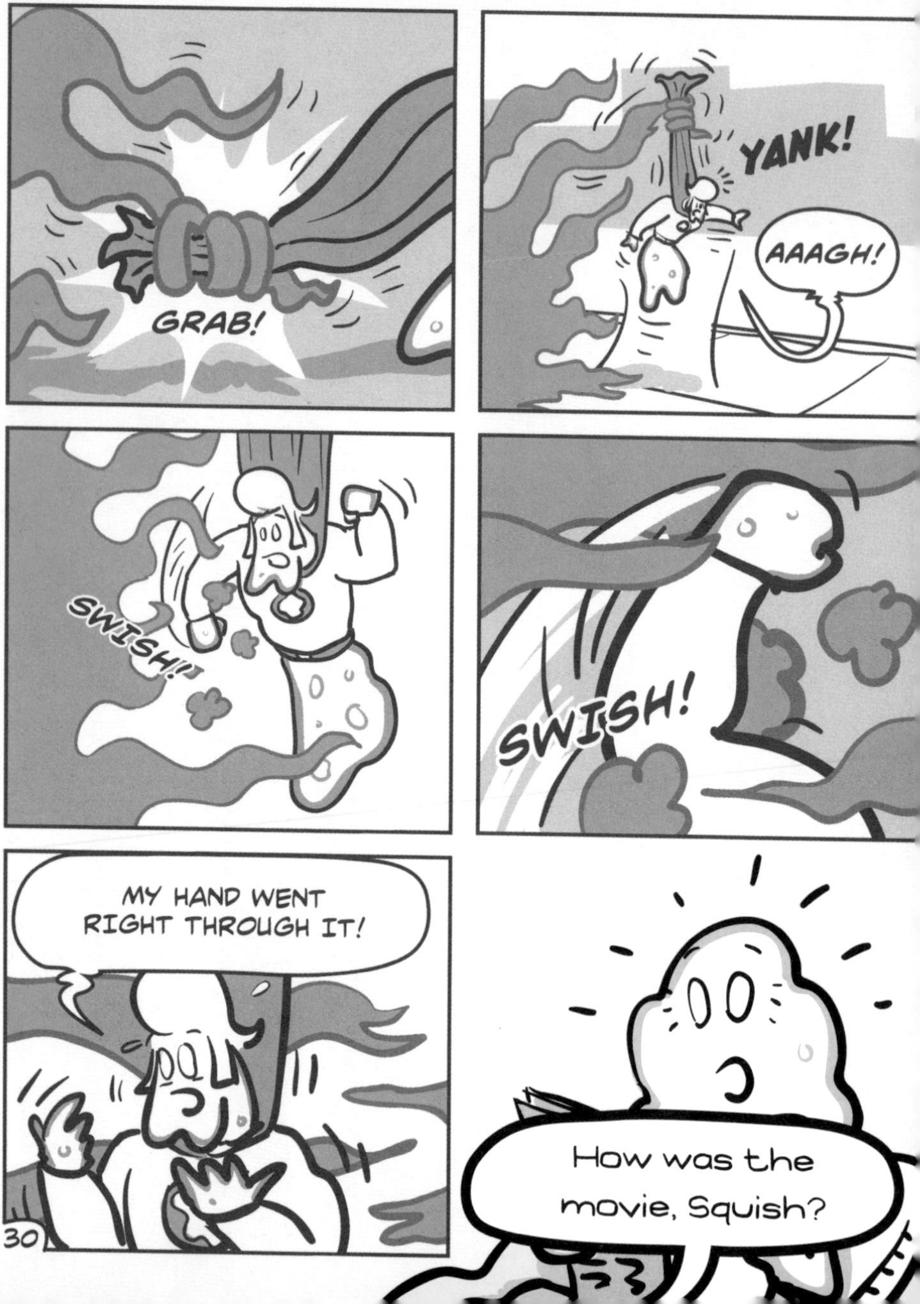
GRAB!
YANK!
AAAGH!
SWISH!!
SWISH!
MY HAND WENT RIGHT THROUGH IT!
How was the movie, Squish?

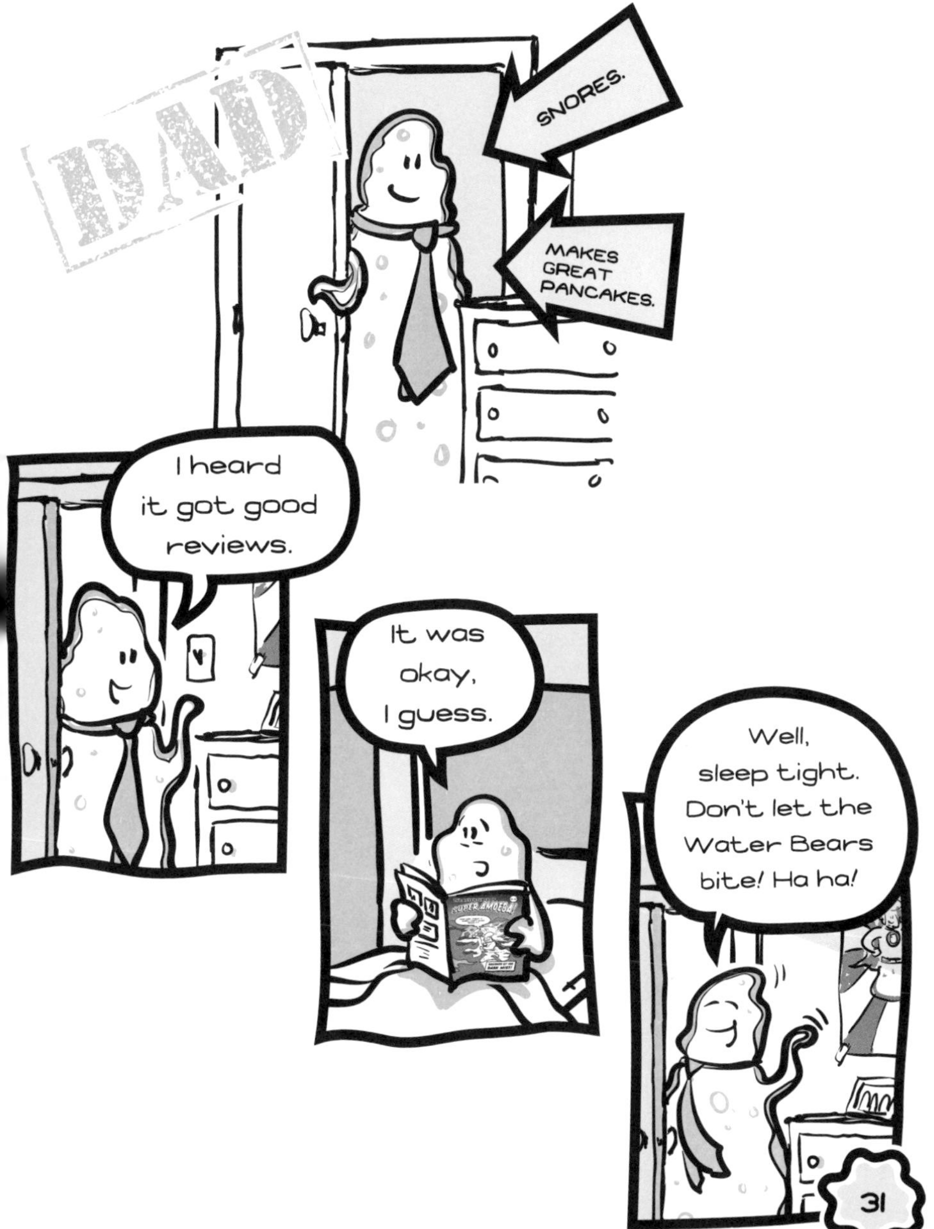
DAD
SNORES.
MAKES GREAT PANCAKES.
I heard it got good reviews.
It was okay, I guess.
SUPER AMOEBA!
Well, sleep tight. Don't let the Water Bears bite! Ha ha!

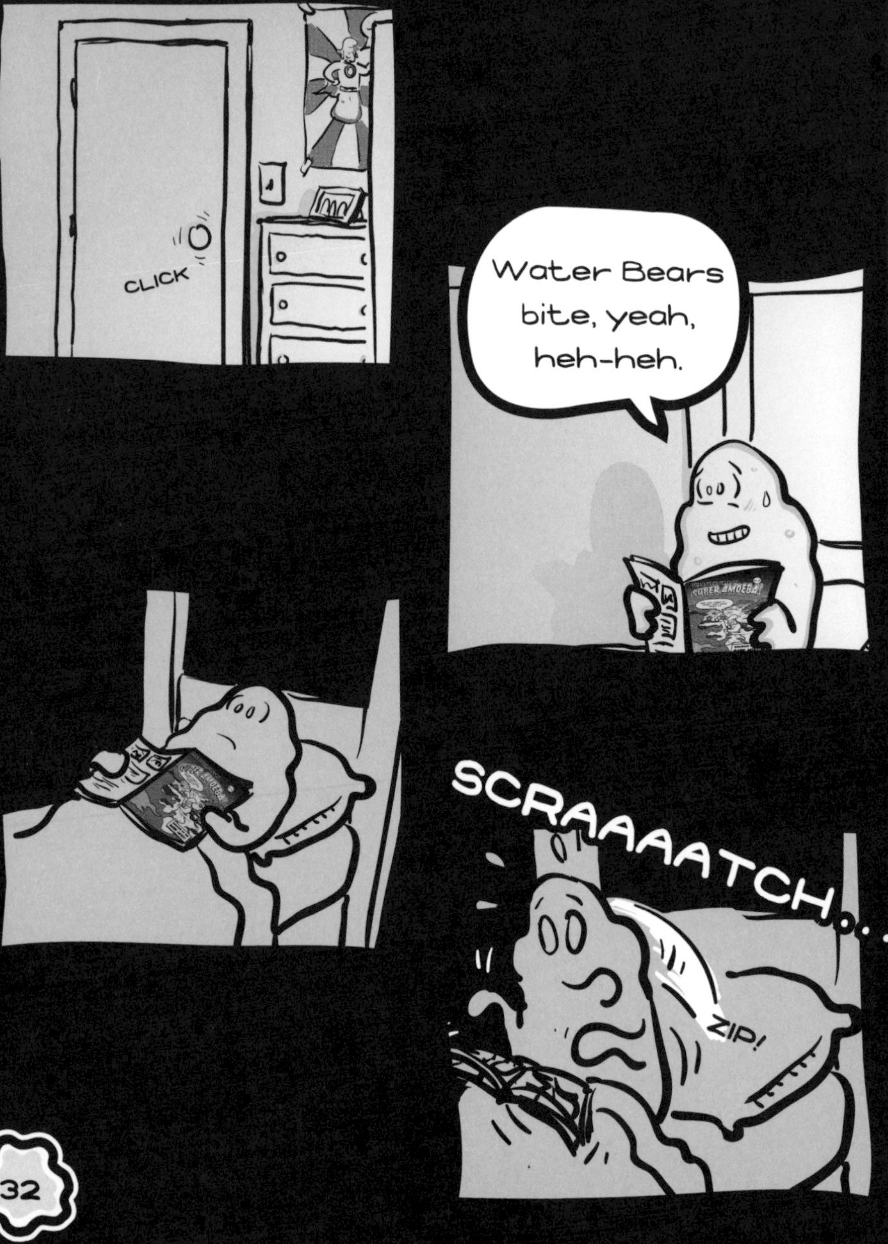
CLICK
Water Bears bite, yeah, heh-heh.
SCRAAAATCH...
ZIP!

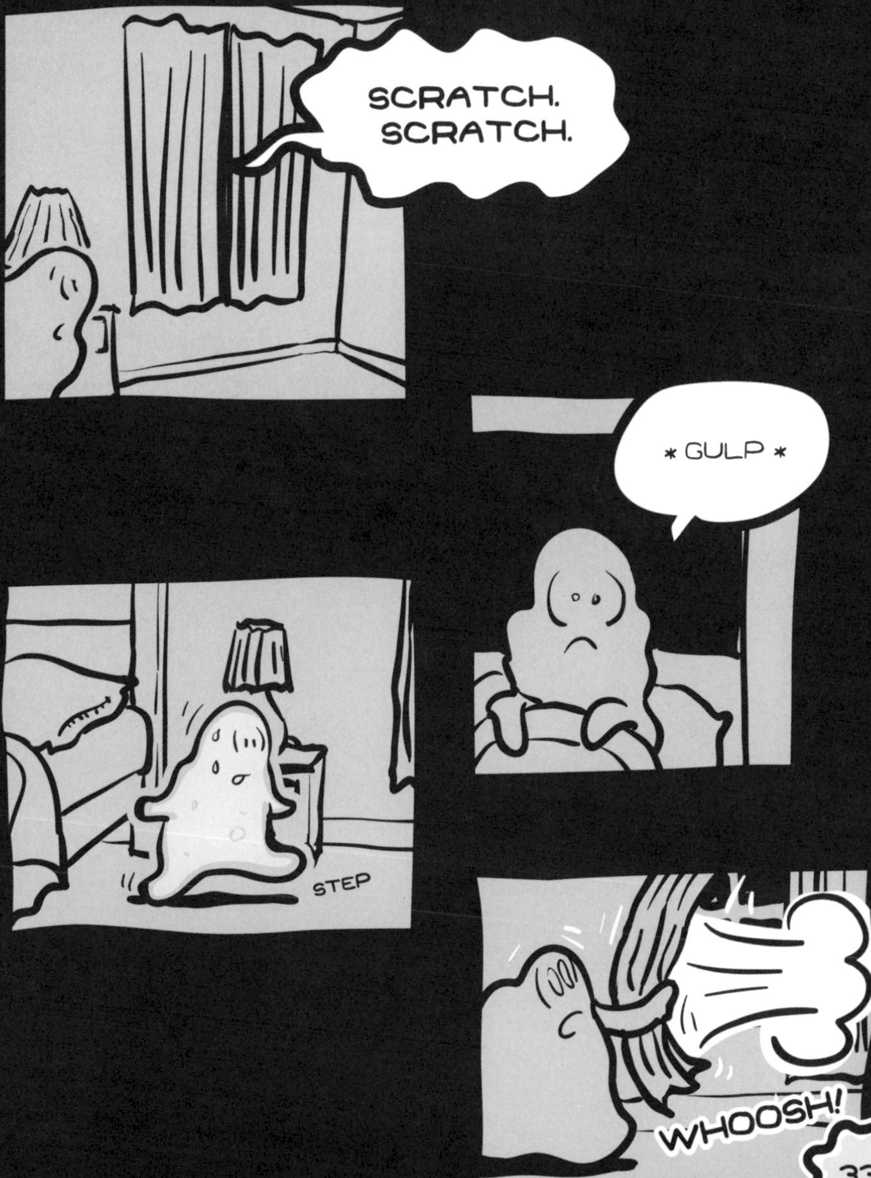

SCRATCH.
SCRATCH.
* GULP *
STEP
WHOOSH!

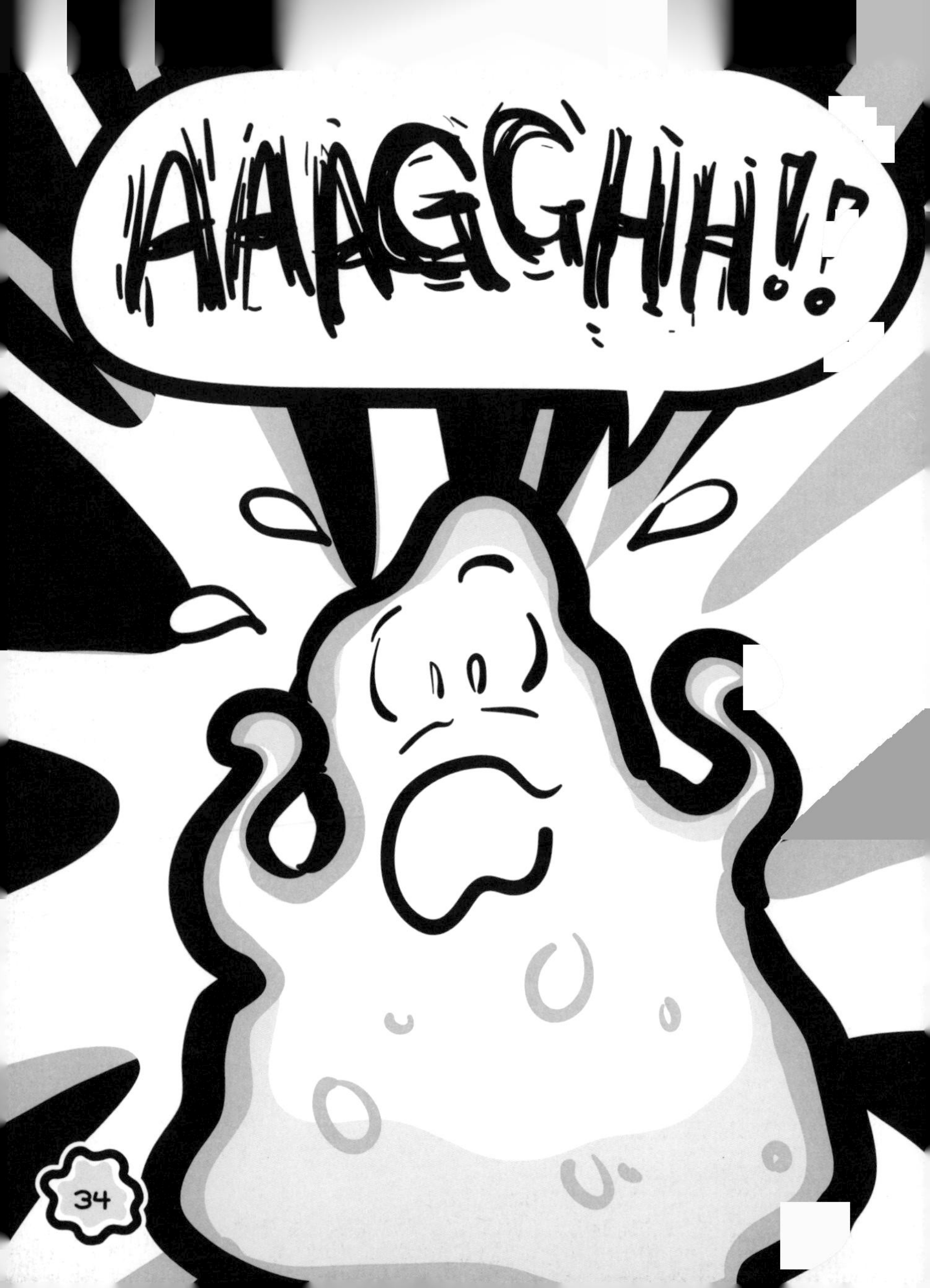
AAGGHH!!

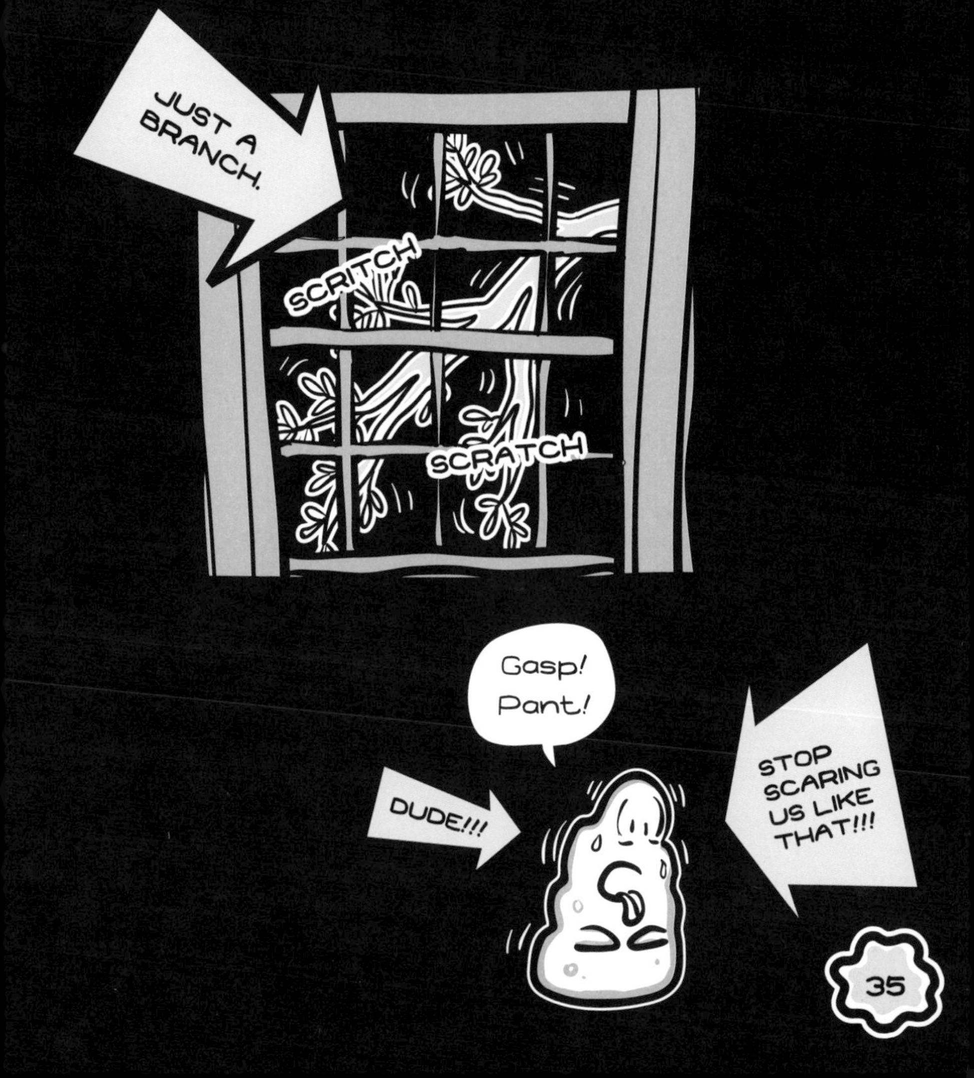
JUST A BRANCH.
SCRITCH
SCRATCH
Gasp! Pant!
DUDE!!!
STOP SCARING US LIKE THAT!!!

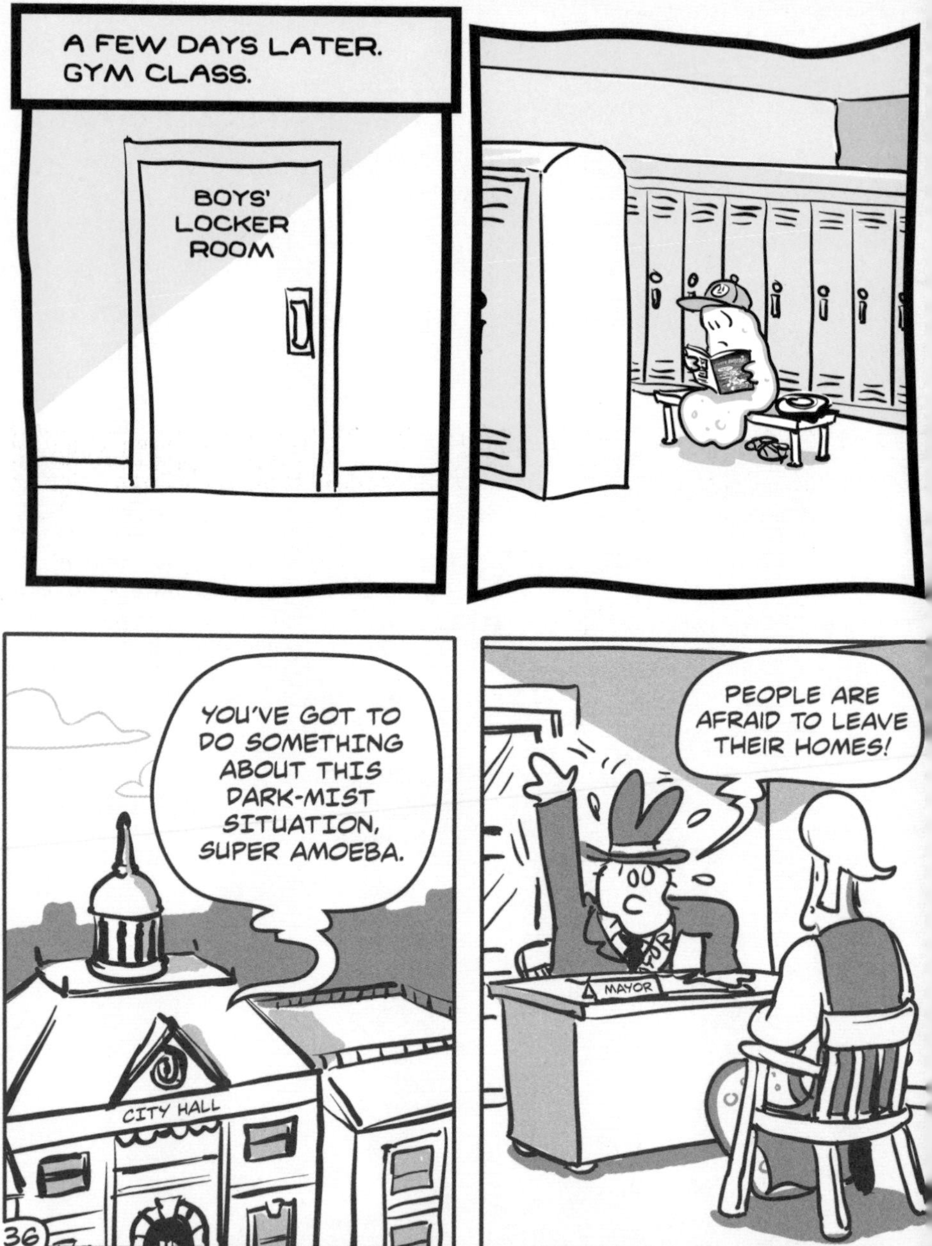
A FEW DAYS LATER.
GYM CLASS.
BOYS' LOCKER ROOM
YOU'VE GOT TO DO SOMETHING ABOUT THIS DARK-MIST SITUATION, SUPER AMOEBA.
CITY HALL
PEOPLE ARE AFRAID TO LEAVE THEIR HOMES!
MAYOR

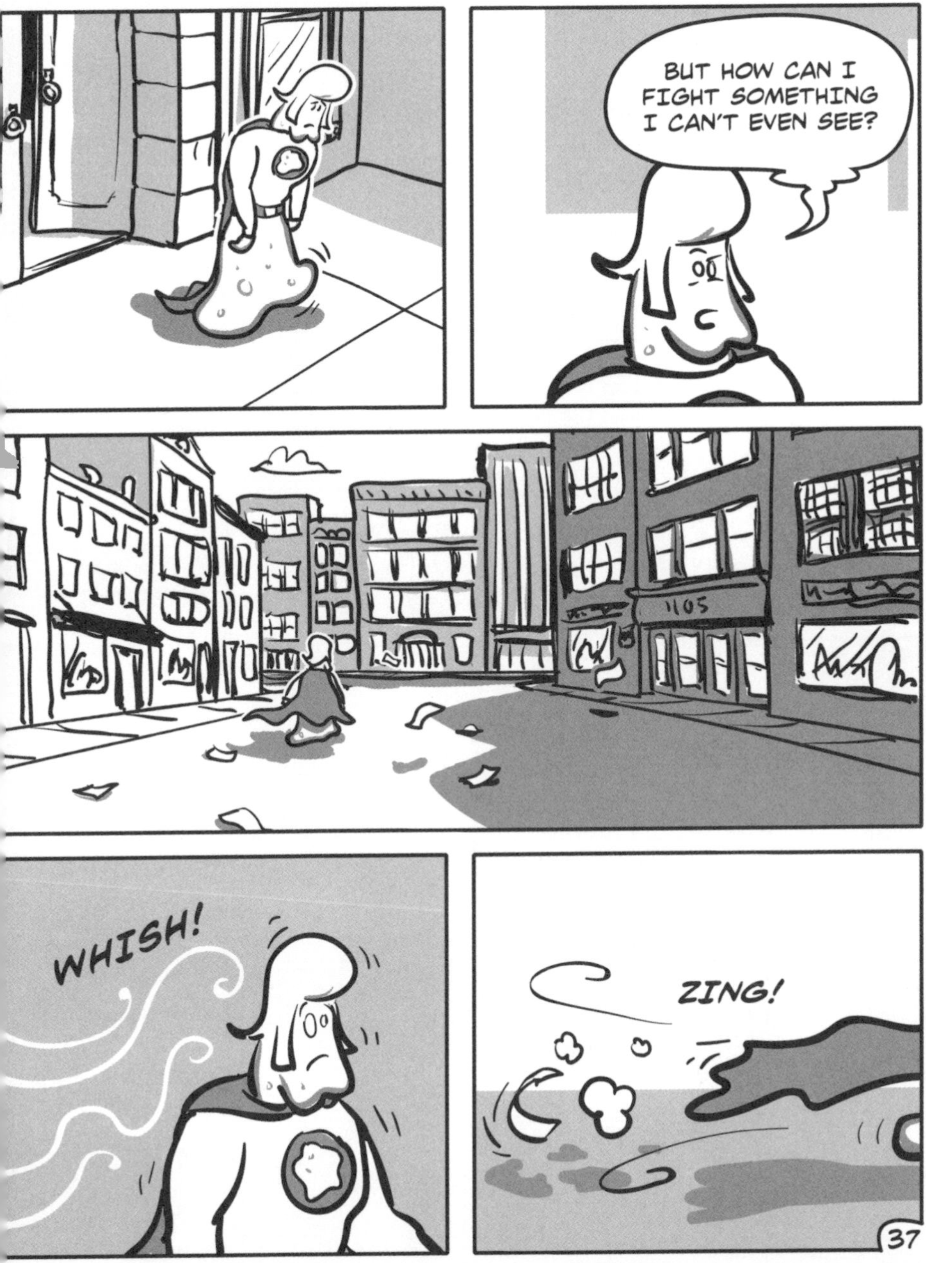
BUT HOW CAN I FIGHT SOMETHING I CAN'T EVEN SEE?
1105
WHISH!
ZING!

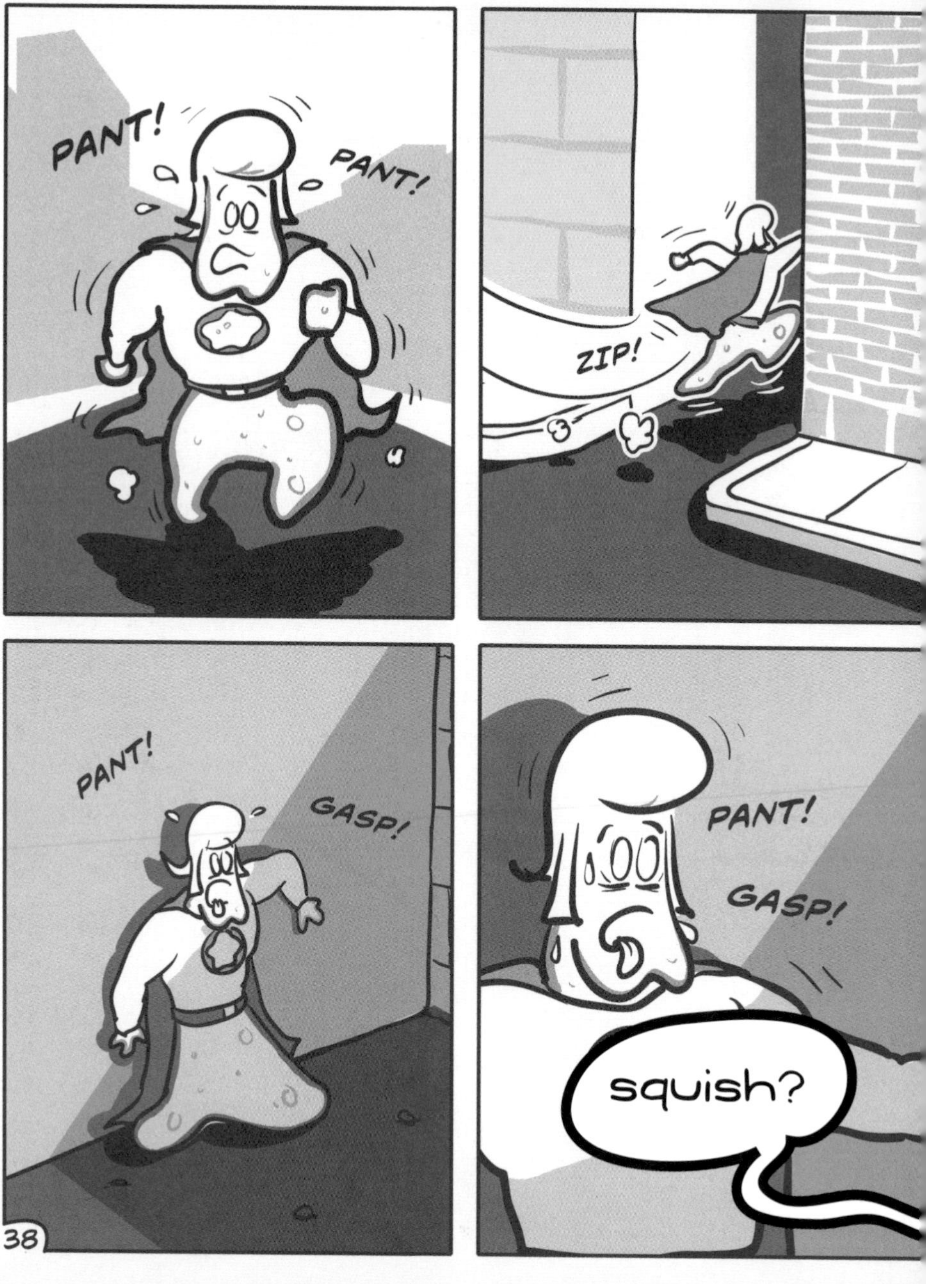
PANT!
PANT!
ZIP!
PANT!
GASP!
PANT!
GASP!
squish?

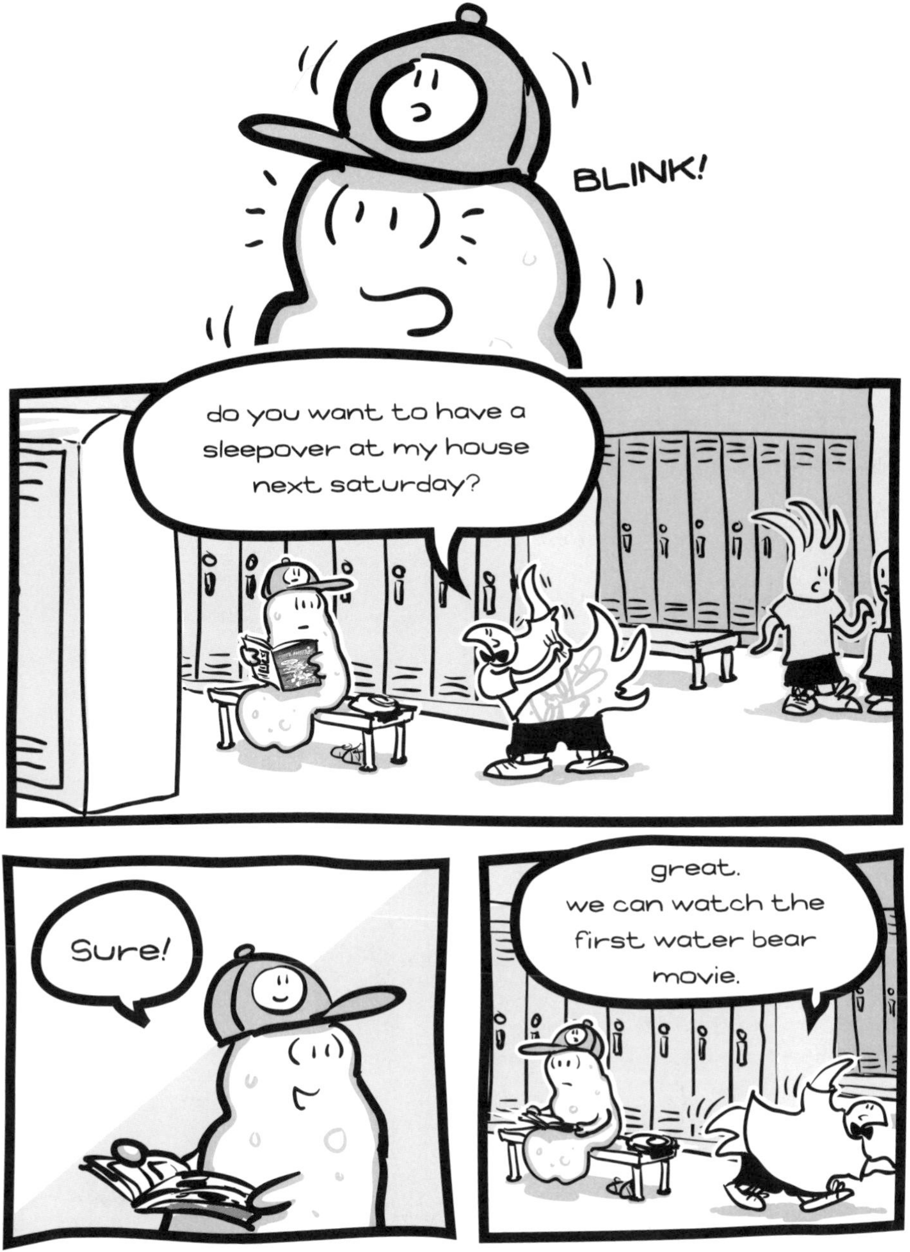
BLINK!
do you want to have a sleepover at my house next saturday?
Sure!
great. we can watch the first water bear movie.

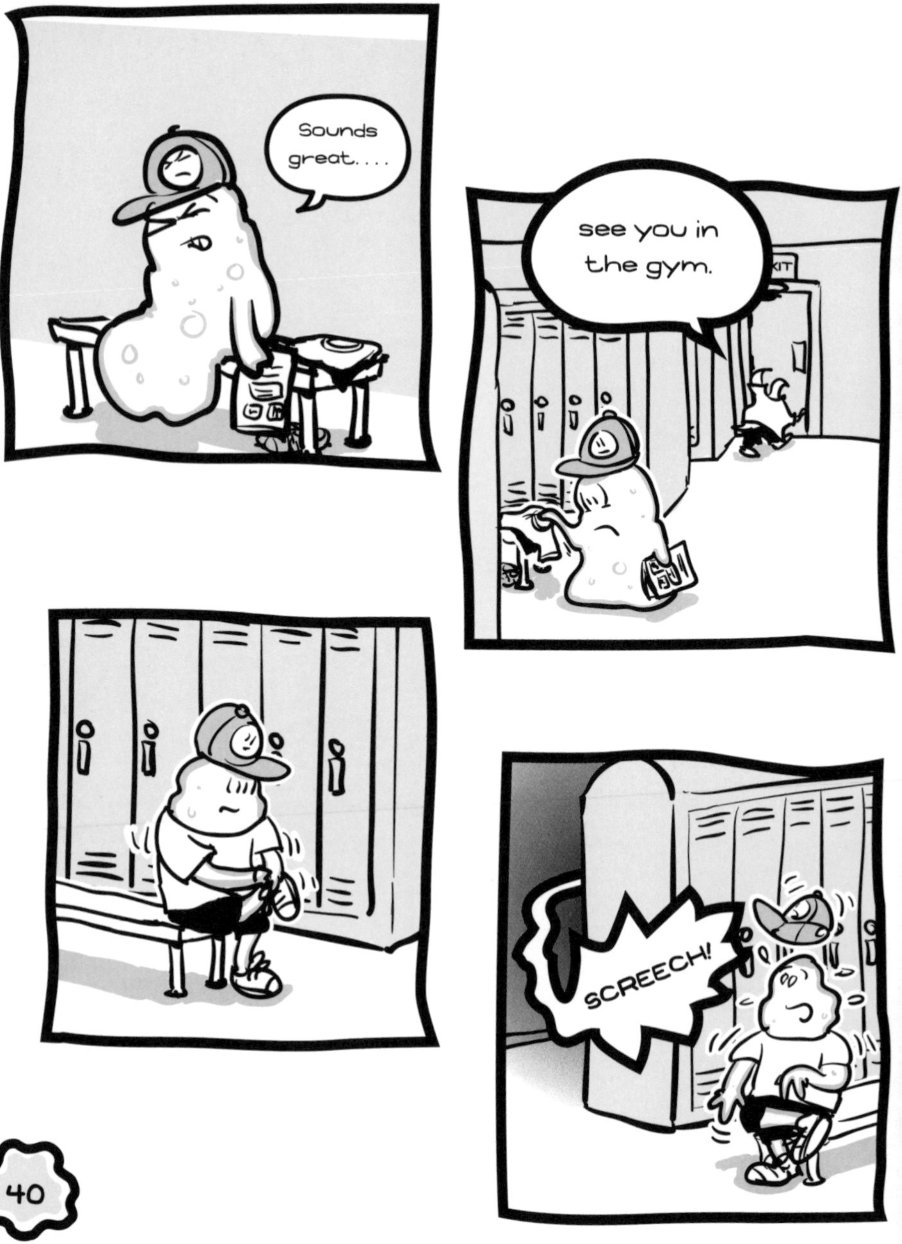
Sounds great. . . .
see you in the gym.
KIT
SCREECH!

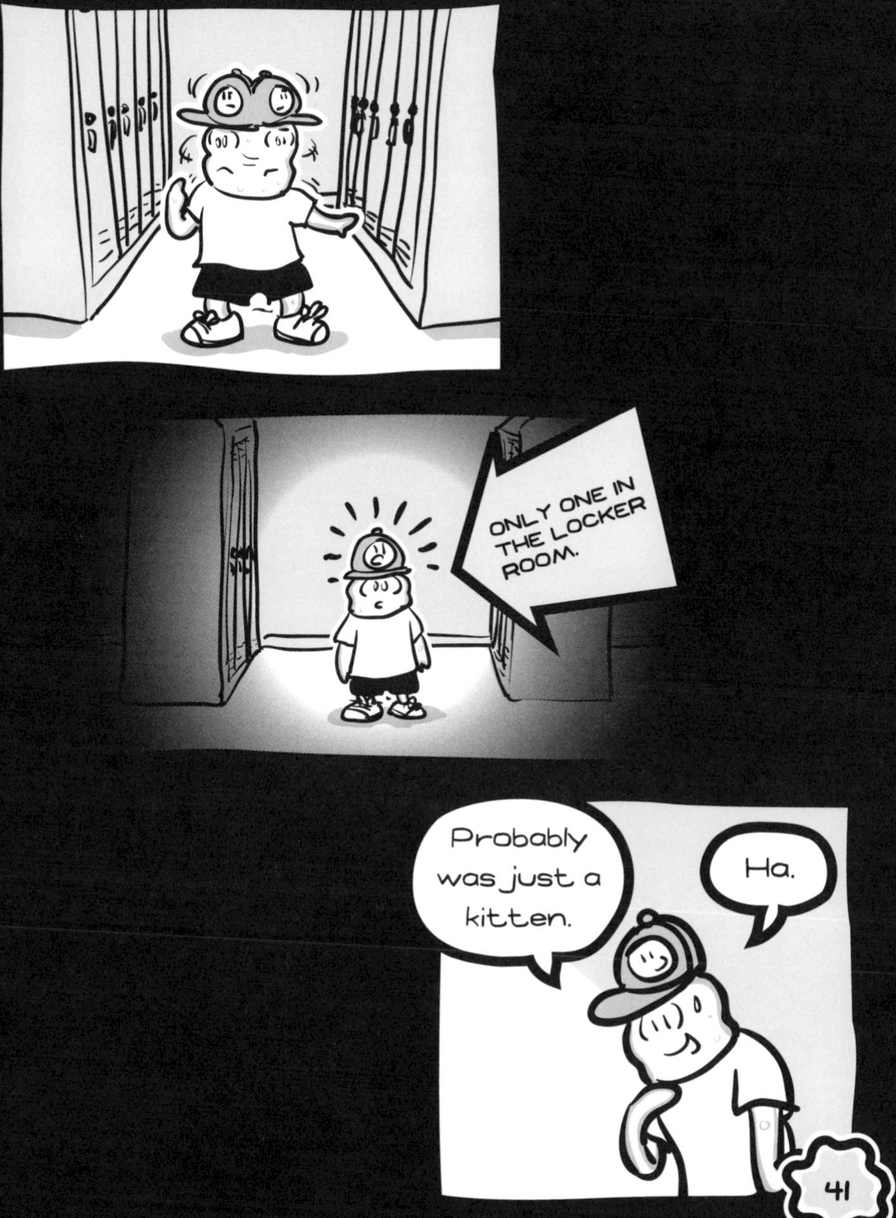
ONLY ONE IN THE LOCKER ROOM.
Probably was just a kitten.
Ha.

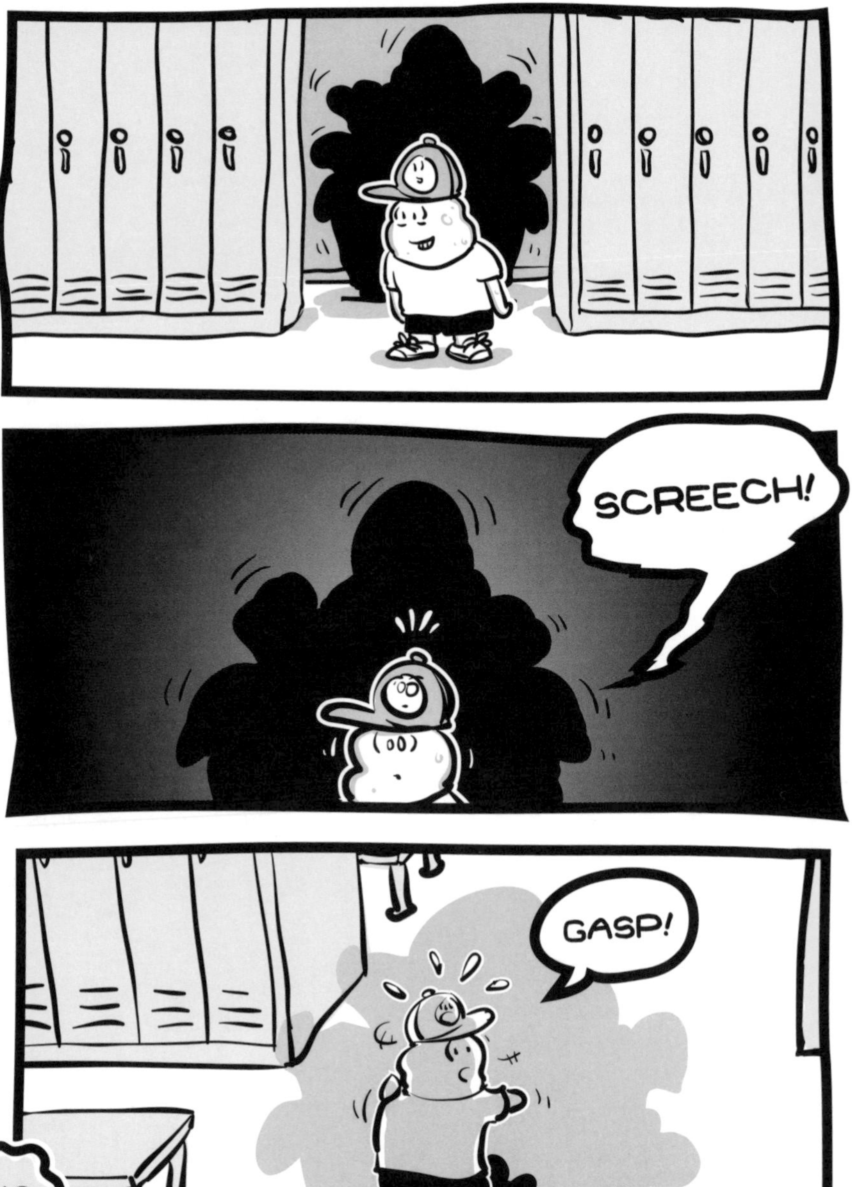
SCREECH!
GASP!

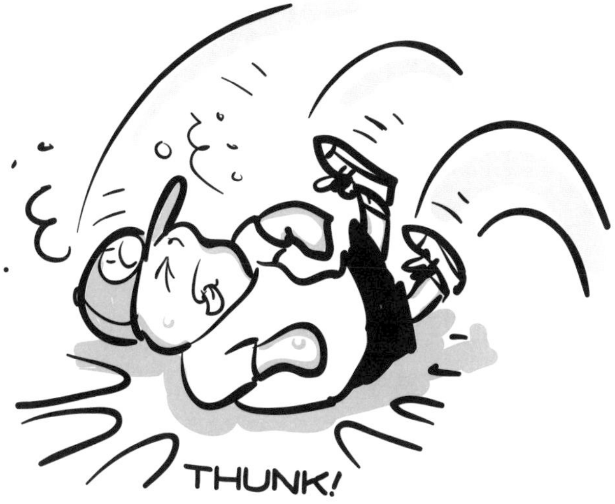
THUNK!

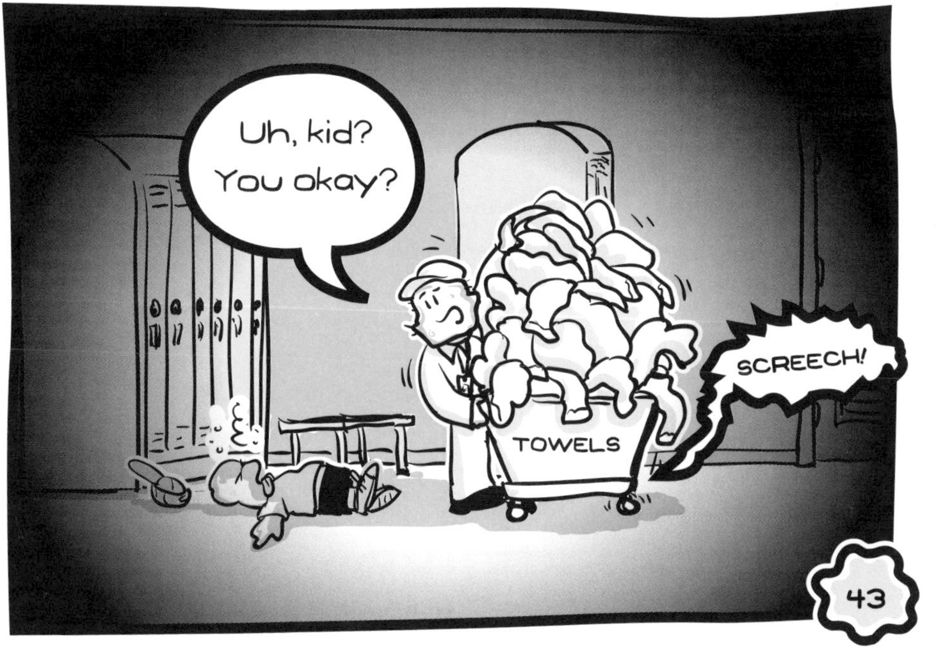
Uh, kid?
You okay?
TOWELS
SCREECH!

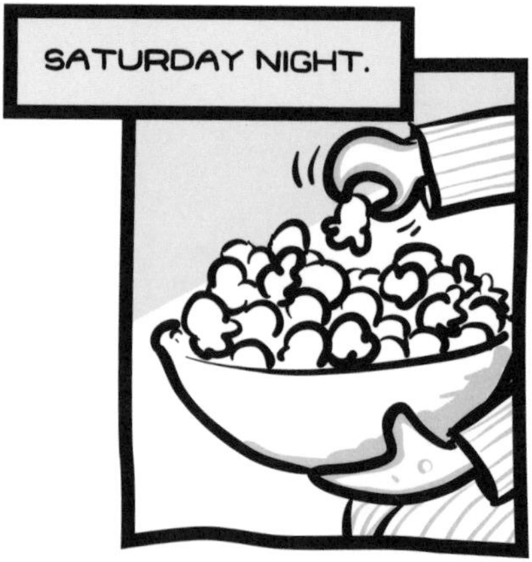
SATURDAY NIGHT.

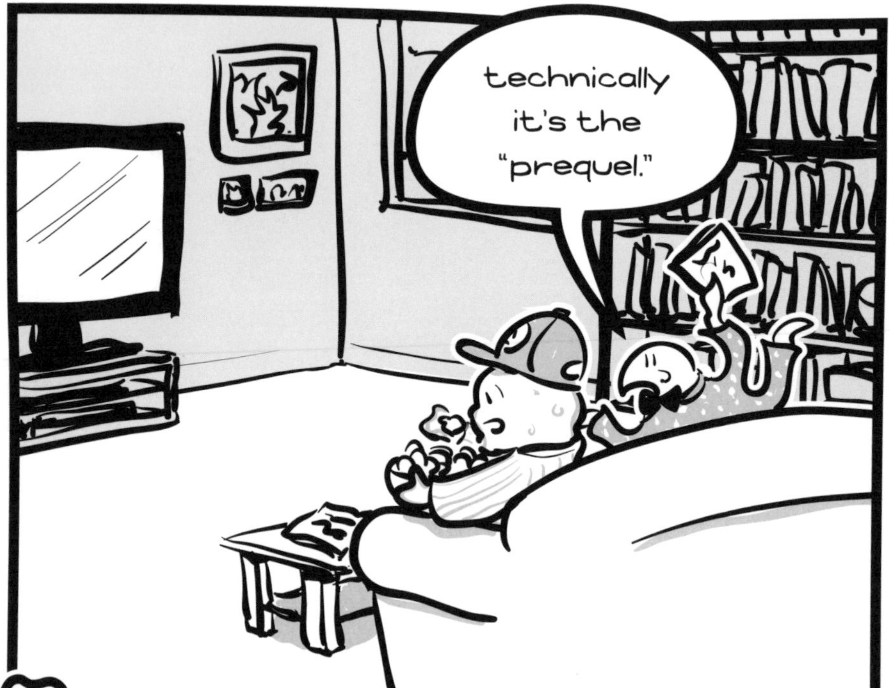
technically it's the "prequel."

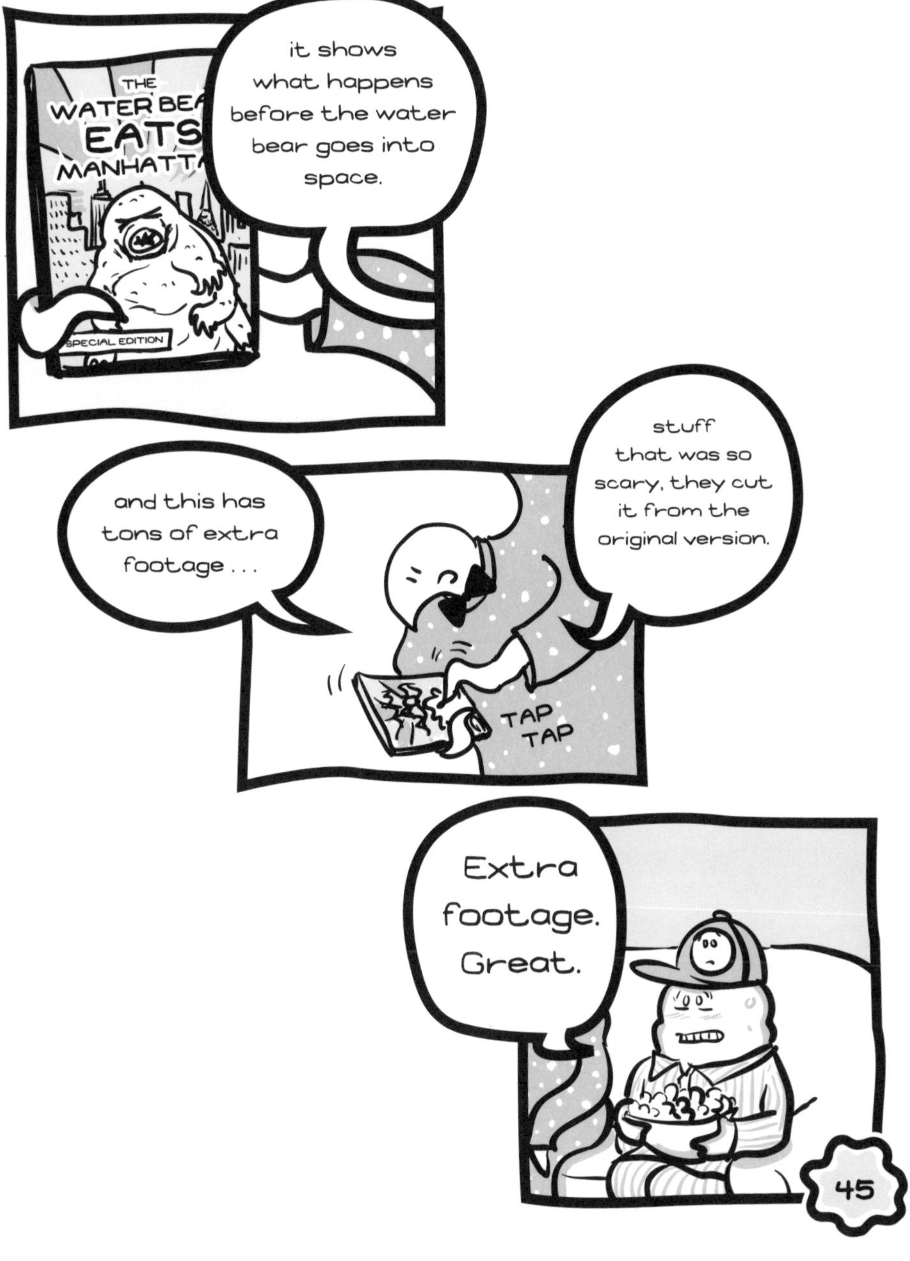
THE
EATS
SPECIAL EDITION
it shows what happens before the water bear goes into space.
and this has tons of extra footage . . .
stuff that was so scary, they cut it from the original version.
TAP TAP
Extra footage. Great.

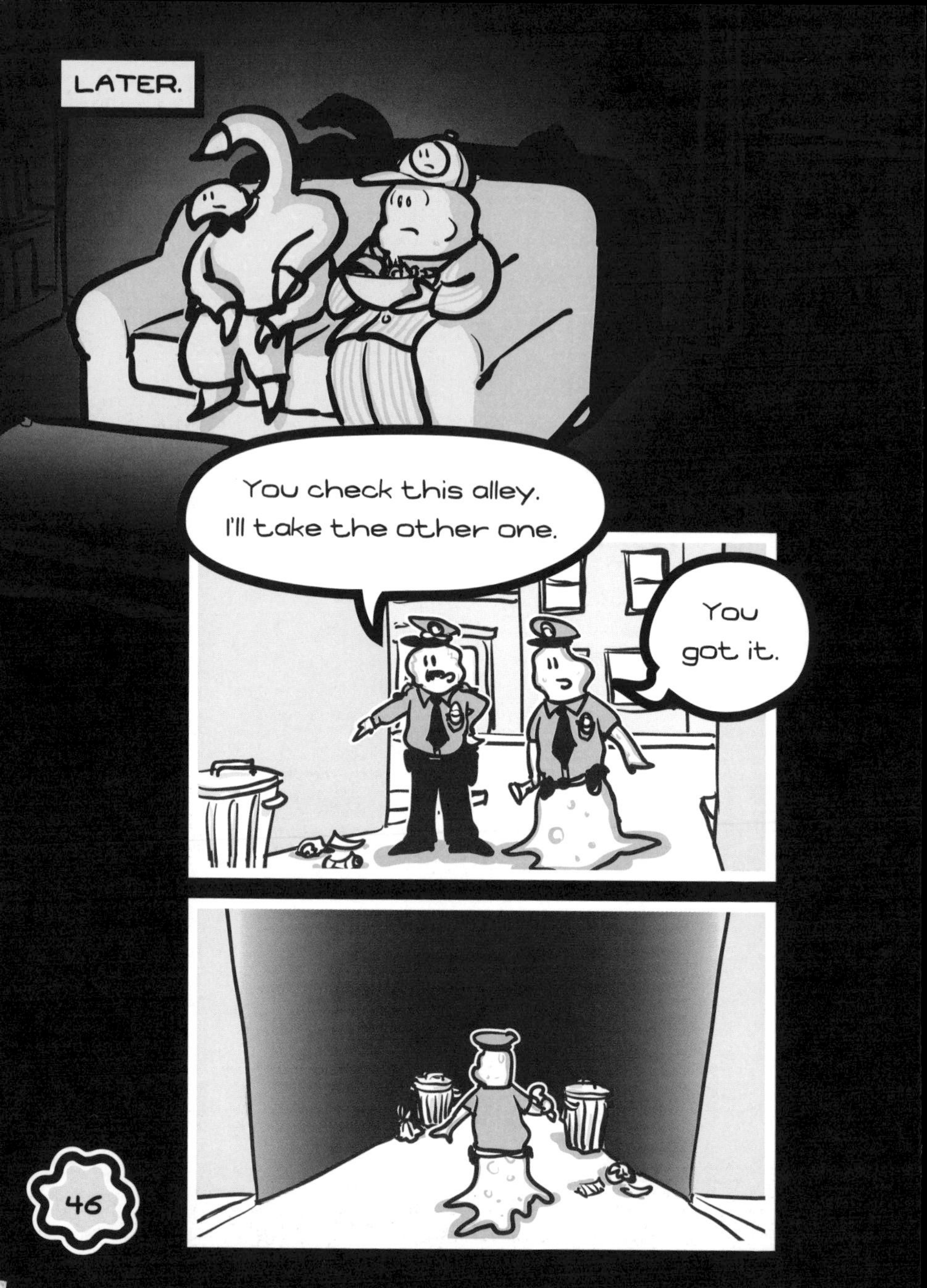
LATER.
You check this alley. I'll take the other one.
You got it.

STEP
STEP
Anything?
RATTLE!
MEOW!
SPROING!

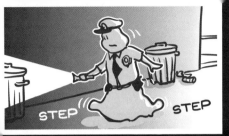

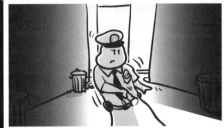

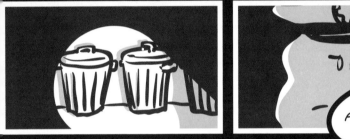

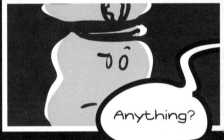

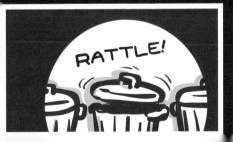

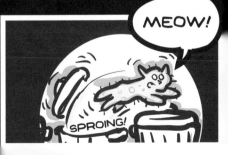

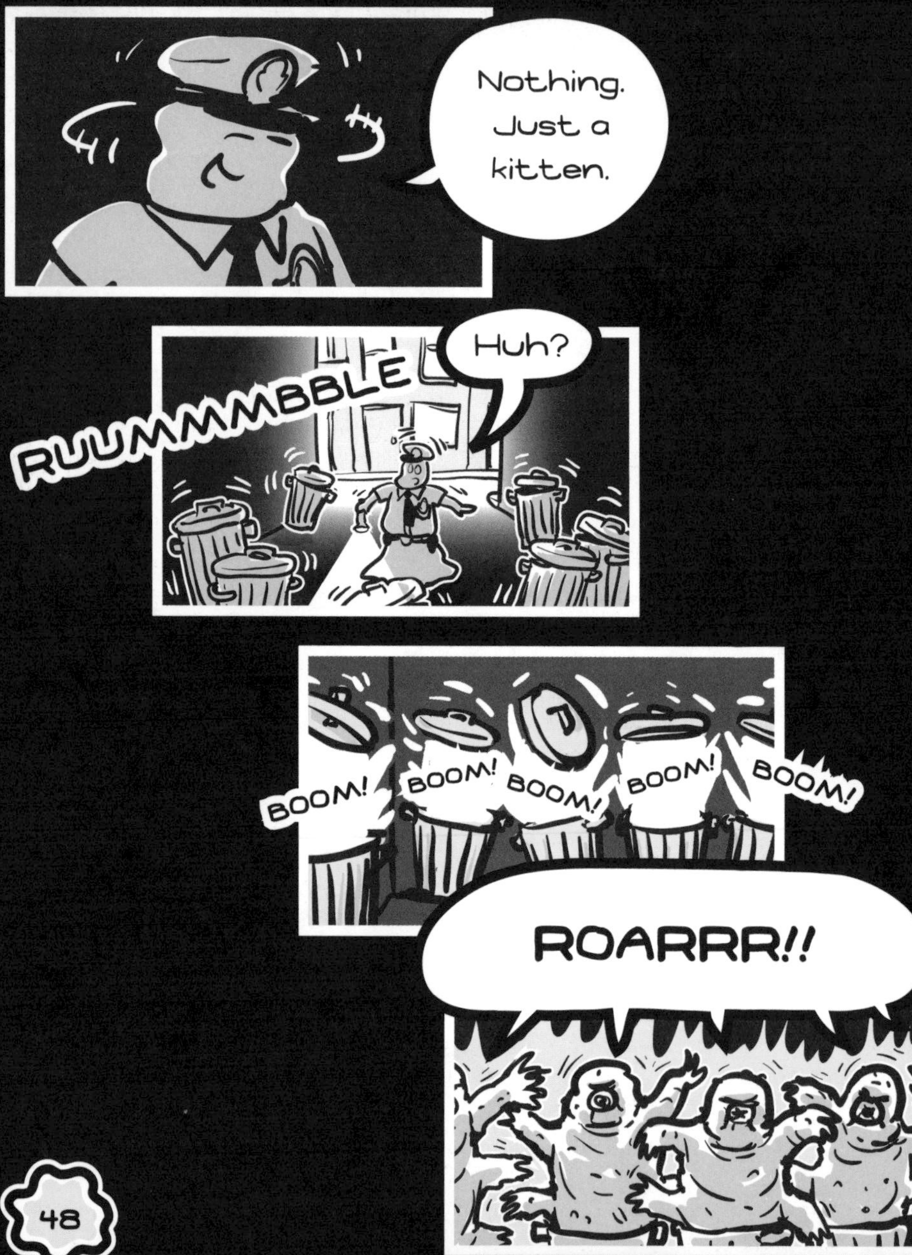
Nothing. Just a kitten.
RUUMMMMBBLE
Huh?
BOOM! BOOM! BOOM! BOOM! BOOM!
ROARRR!!

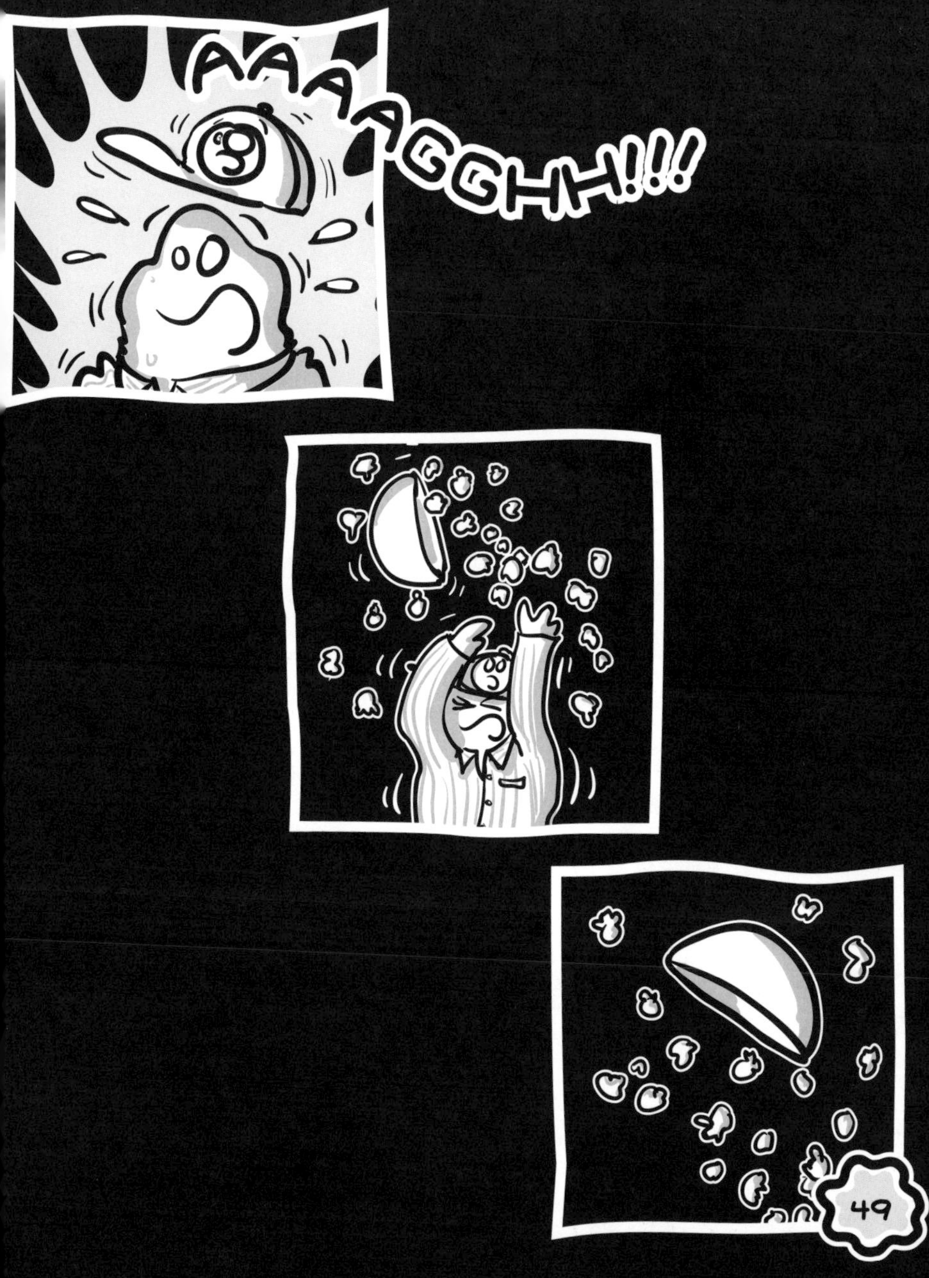
AAAAGGHH!!!

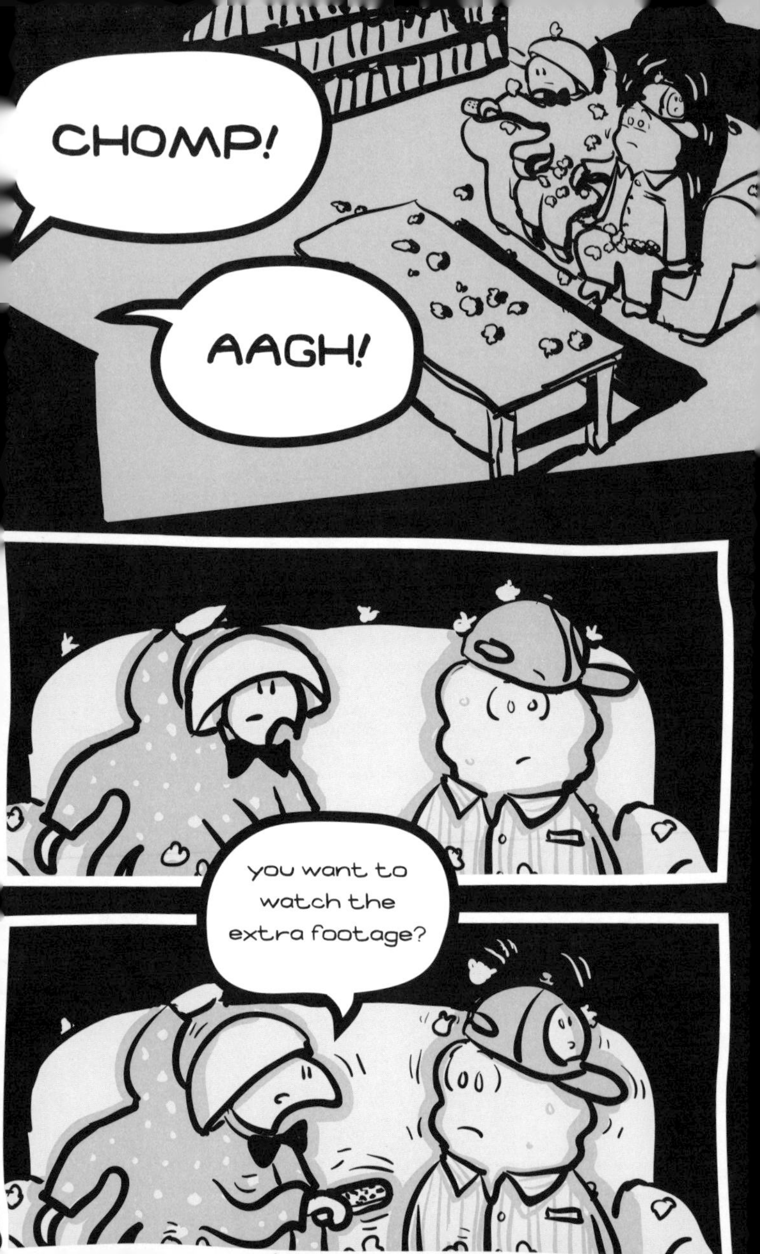
CHOMP!
AAGH!
you want to watch the extra footage?

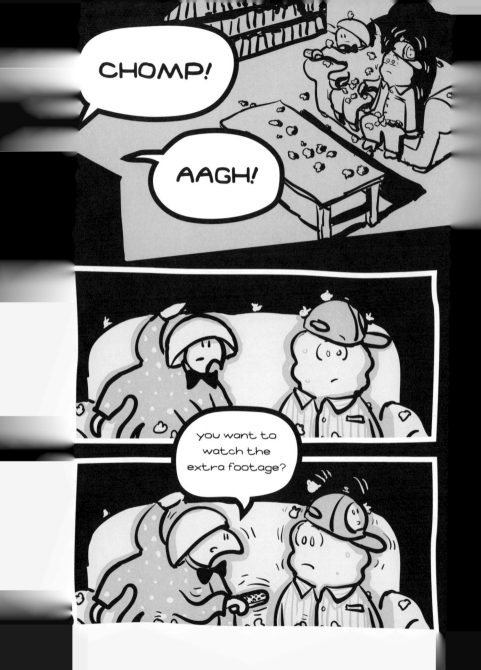

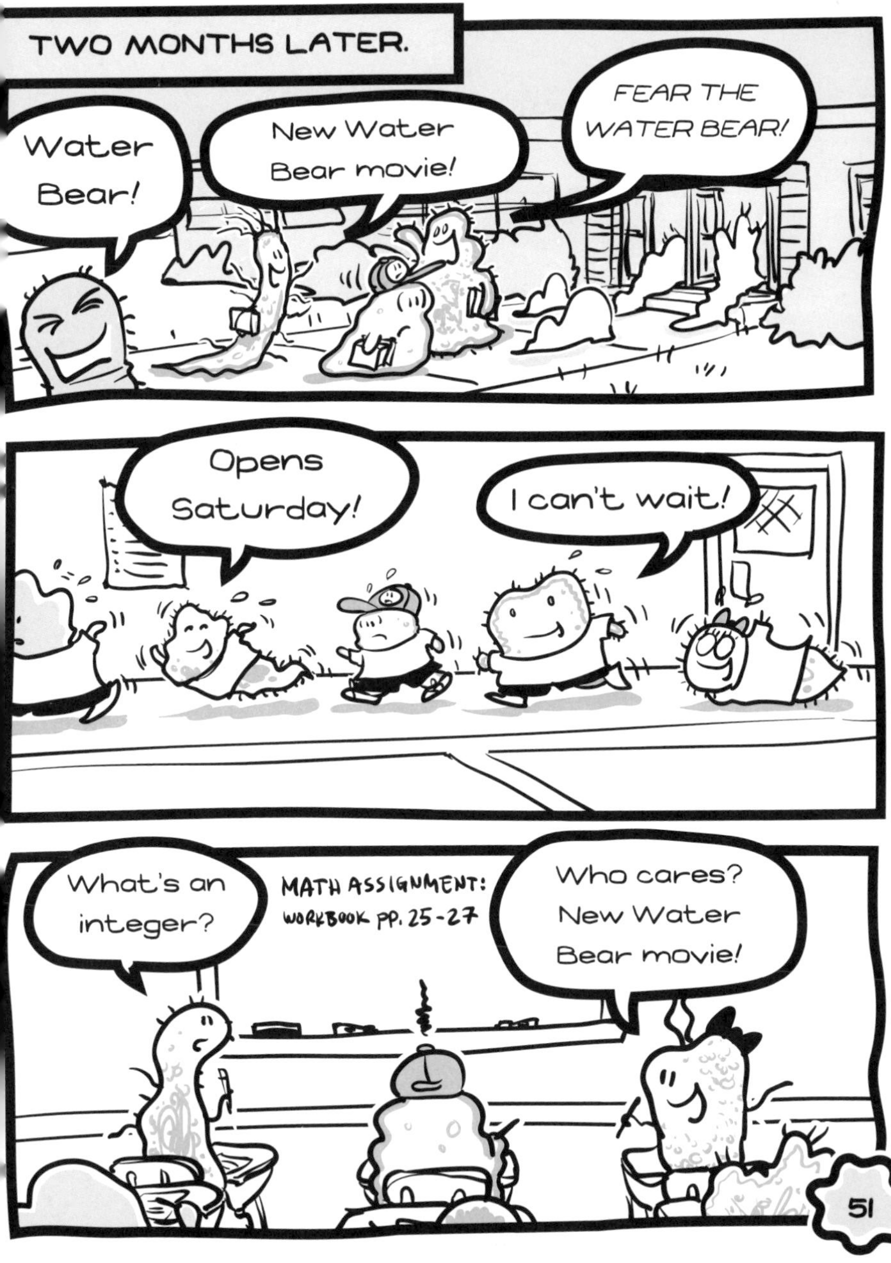
TWO MONTHS LATER.
Water Bear!
New Water Bear movie!
FEAR THE WATER BEAR!
Opens Saturday!
I can't wait!
What's an integer?
MATH ASSIGNMENT: WORKBOOK PP. 25-27
Who cares? New Water Bear movie!

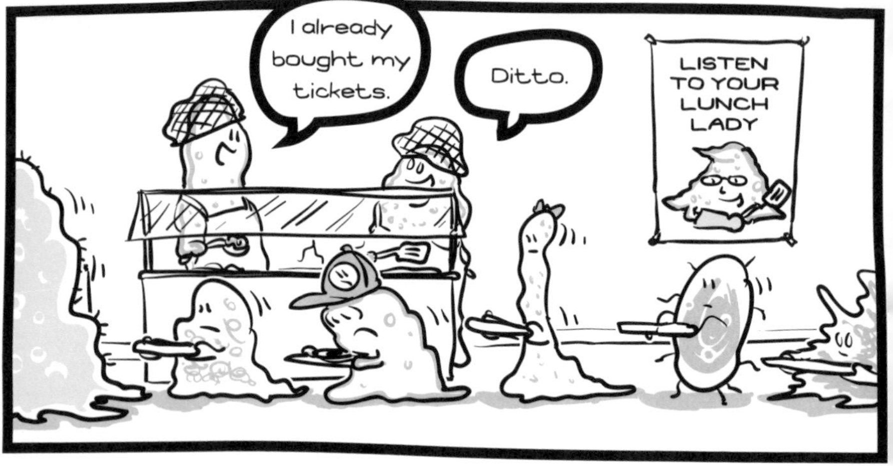
I already bought my tickets.
Ditto.
LISTEN TO YOUR LUNCH LADY

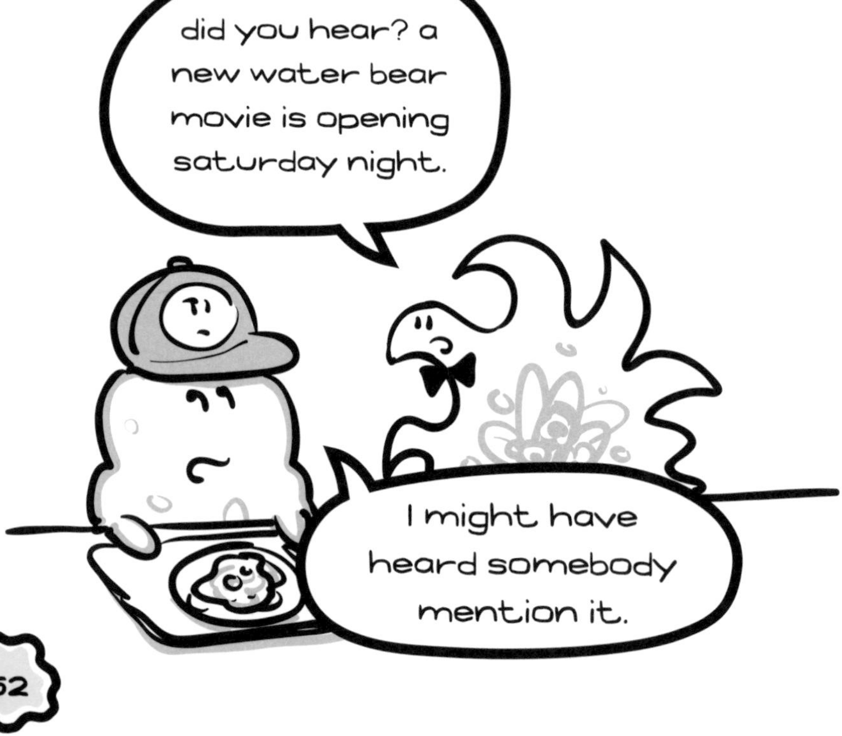
did you hear? a new water bear movie is opening saturday night.
I might have heard somebody mention it.

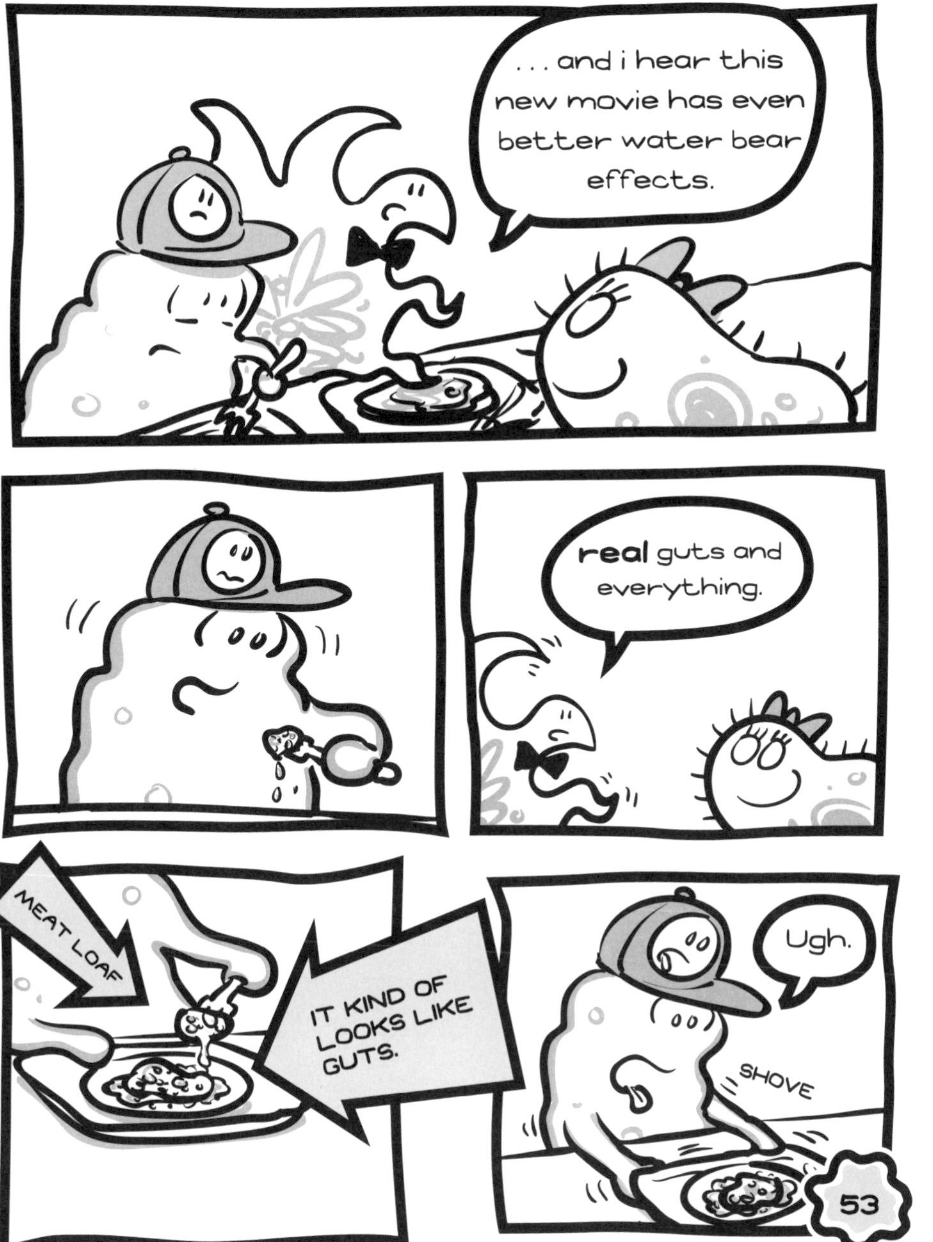
. . . and i hear this new movie has even better water bear effects.
real guts and everything.
MEAT LOAF
IT KIND OF LOOKS LIKE GUTS.
Ugh.
SHOVE

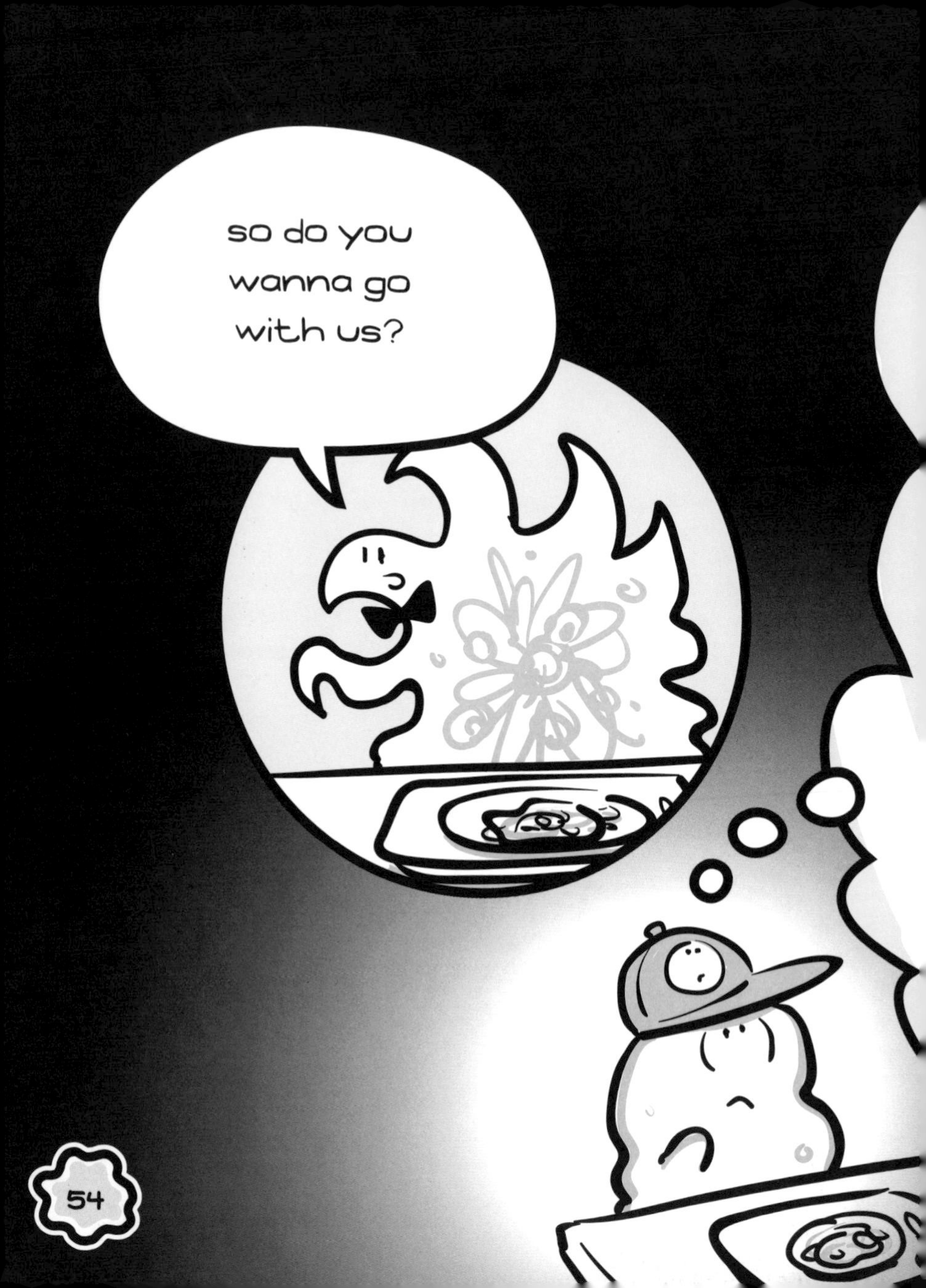
so do you wanna go with us?

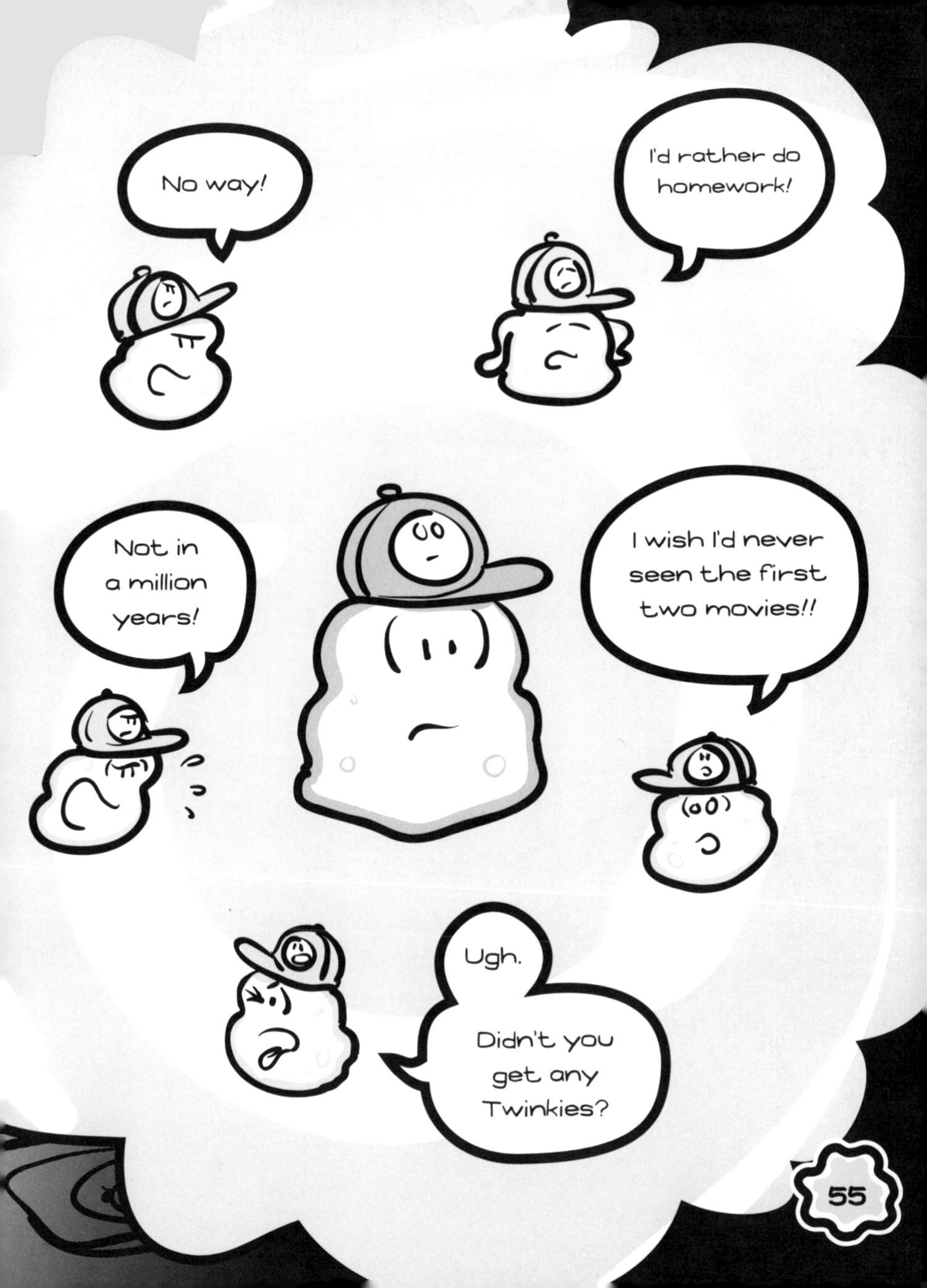
No way!
I'd rather do homework!
Not in a million years!
I wish I'd never seen the first two movies!!
Ugh.
Didn't you get any Twinkies?

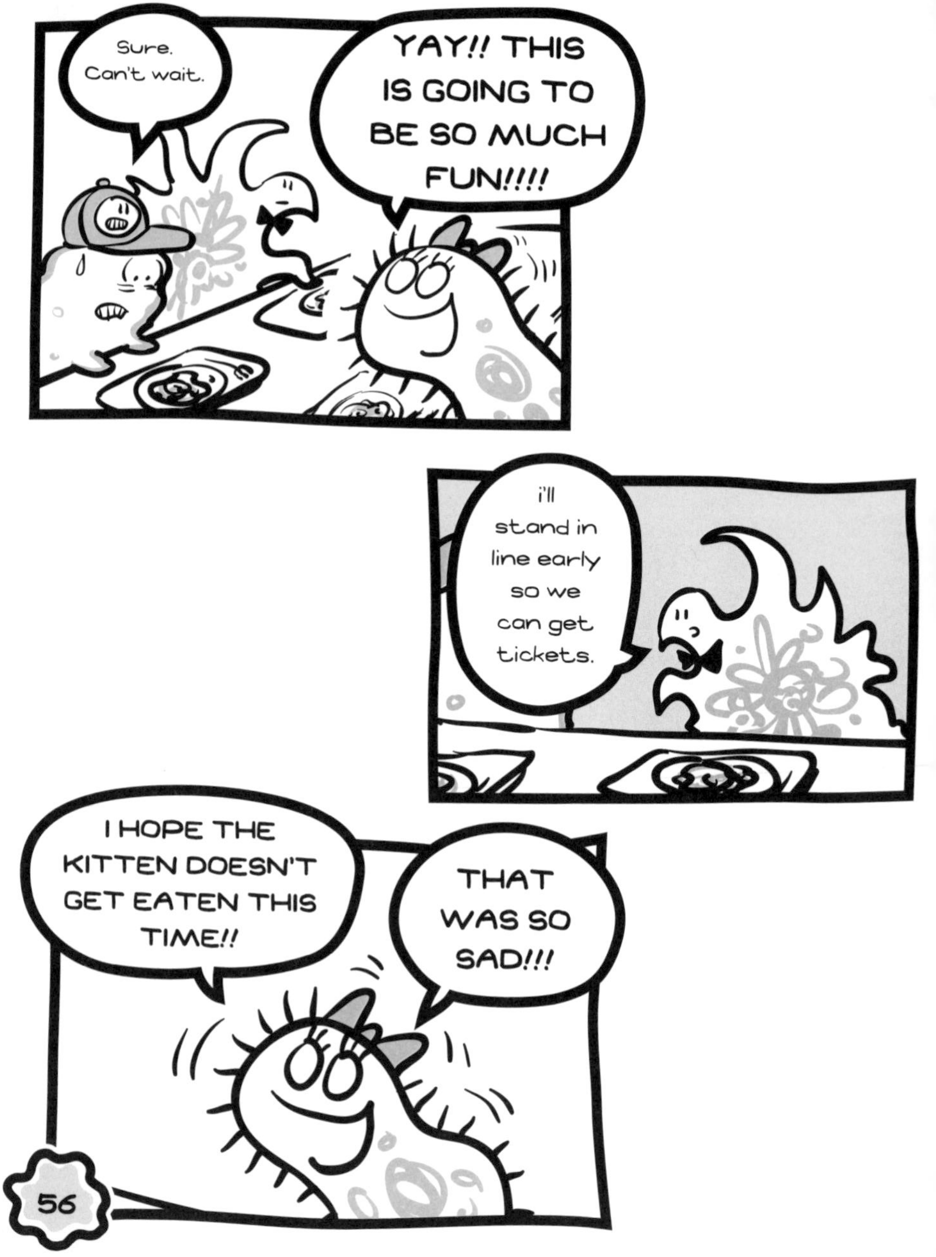

Sure. Can't wait.
YAY!! THIS IS GOING TO BE SO MUCH FUN!!!!
i'll stand in line early so we can get tickets.
I HOPE THE KITTEN DOESN'T GET EATEN THIS TIME!!
THAT WAS SO SAD!!!

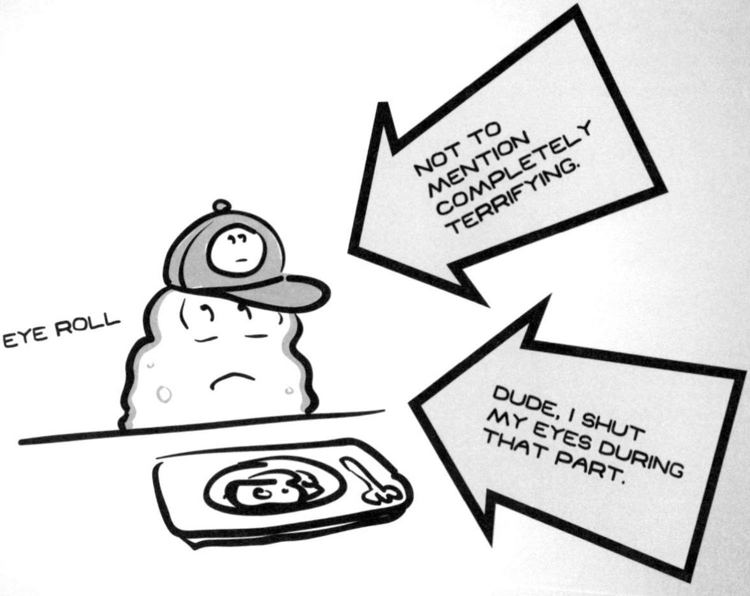
NOT TO MENTION COMPLETELY TERRIFYING.
EYE ROLL
DUDE, I SHUT MY EYES DURING THAT PART.

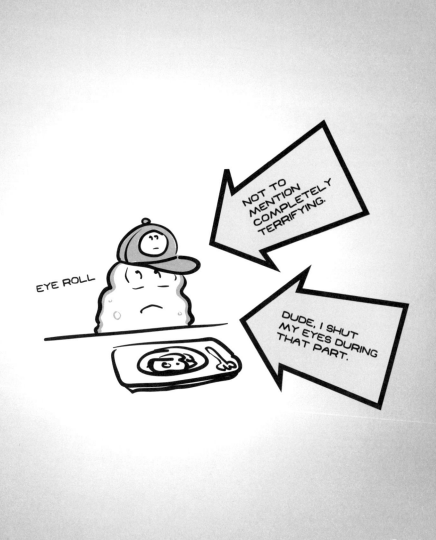

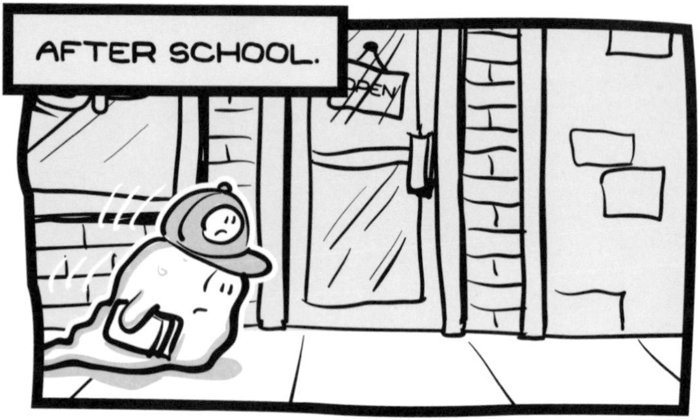
AFTER SCHOOL.
OPEN

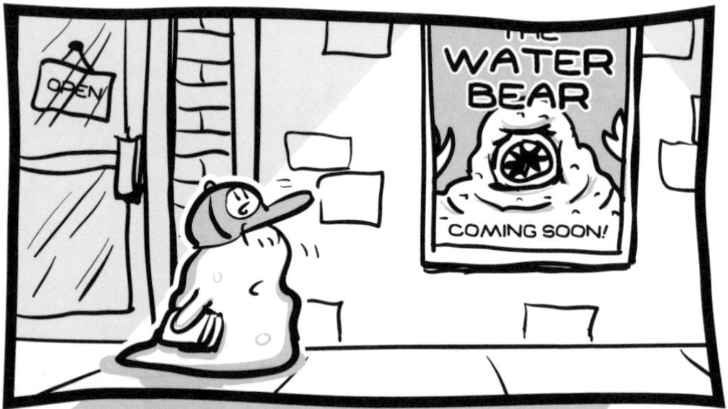
OPEN
WATER
BEAR
COMING SOON!

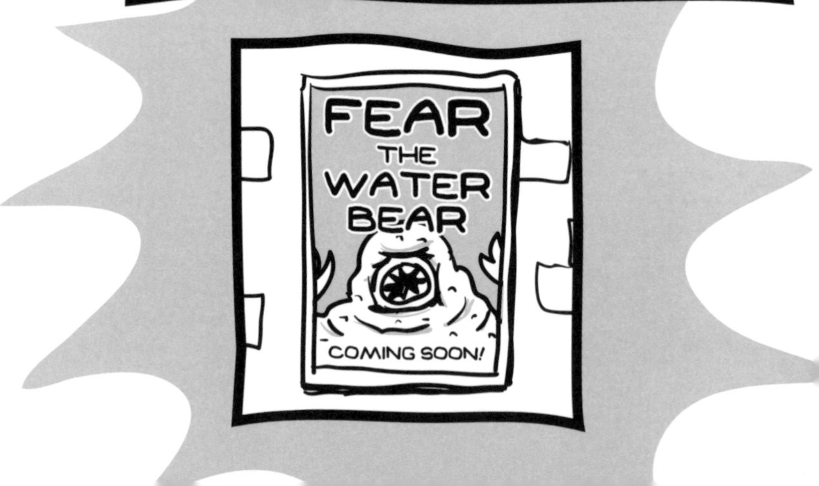
FEAR
THE
WATER
BEAR
COMING SOON!

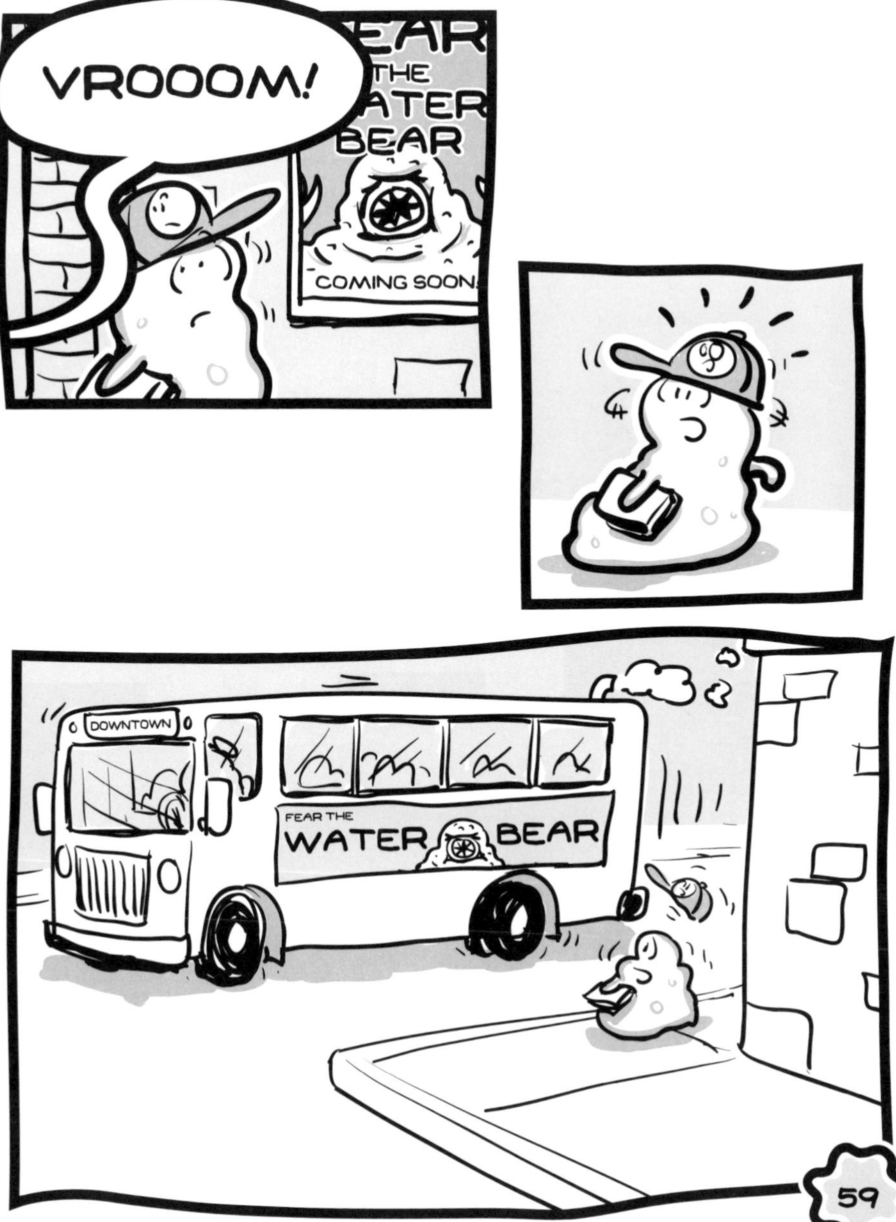
VROOOM!
THE
BEAR
COMING SOON
DOWNTOWN
FEAR THE
WATER BEAR

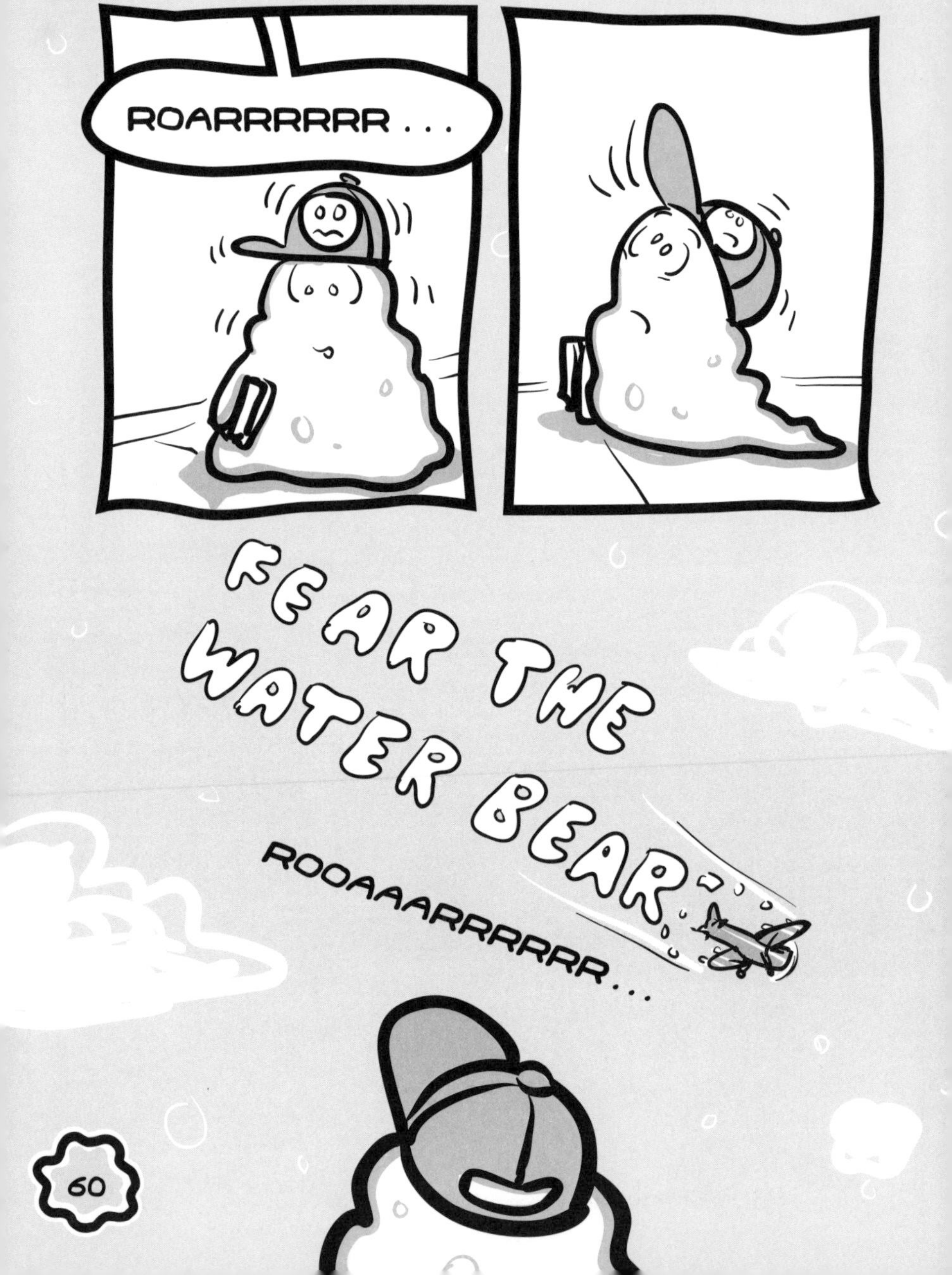
ROARRRRRR . . .
FEAR THE WATER BEAR
ROOAAAARRRRRRR . . .

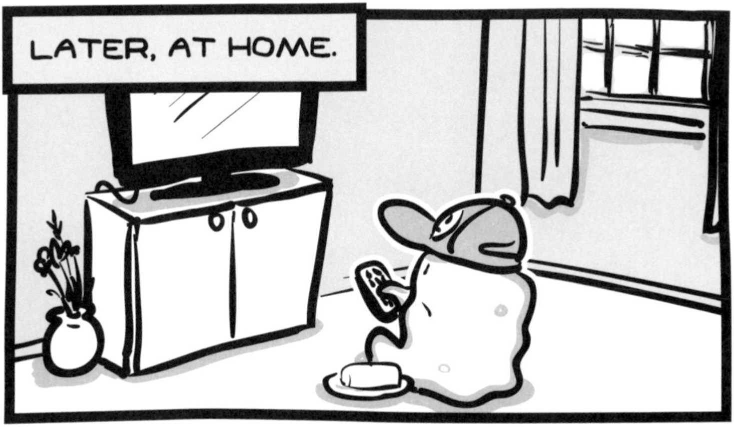
LATER, AT HOME.

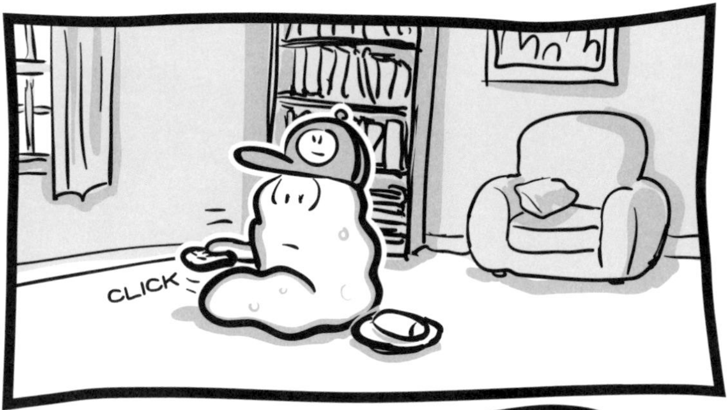
CLICK

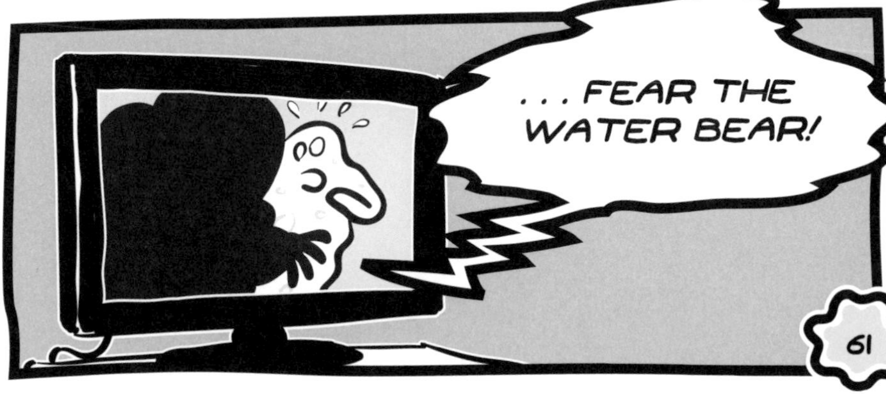
. . . FEAR THE WATER BEAR!

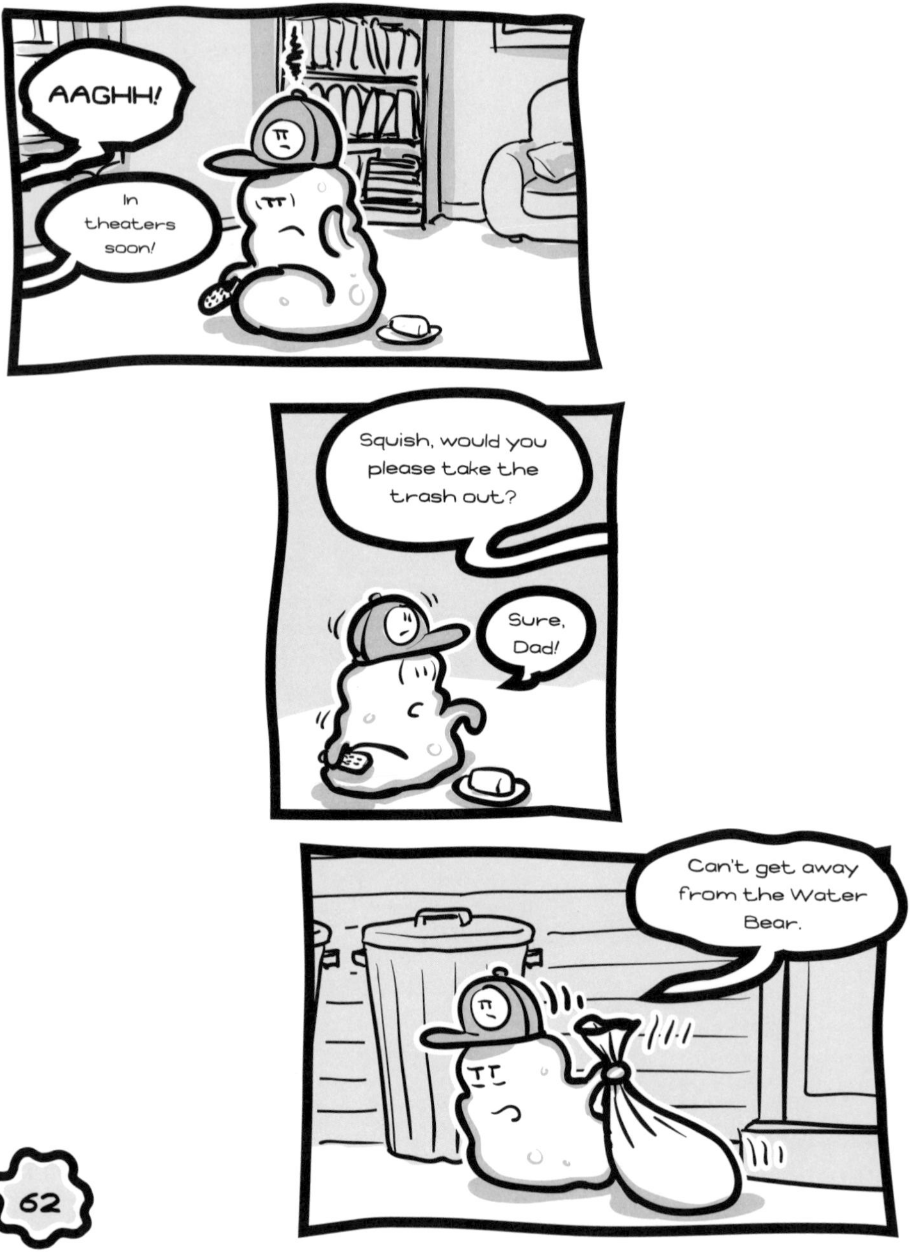
AAGHH!
In theaters soon!
Squish, would you please take the trash out?
Sure, Dad!
Can't get away from the Water Bear.

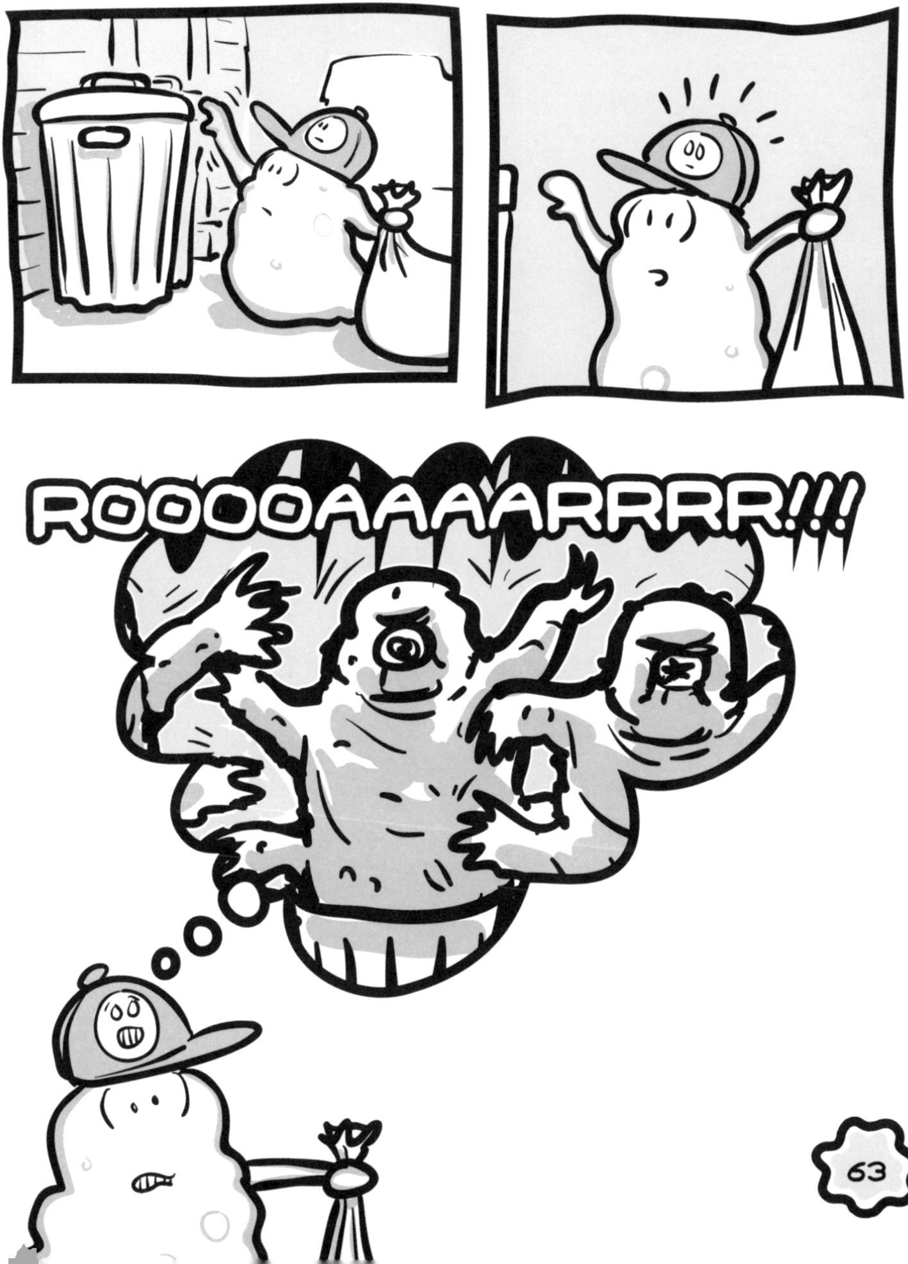
ROOOOAAAAARRRRR!!!

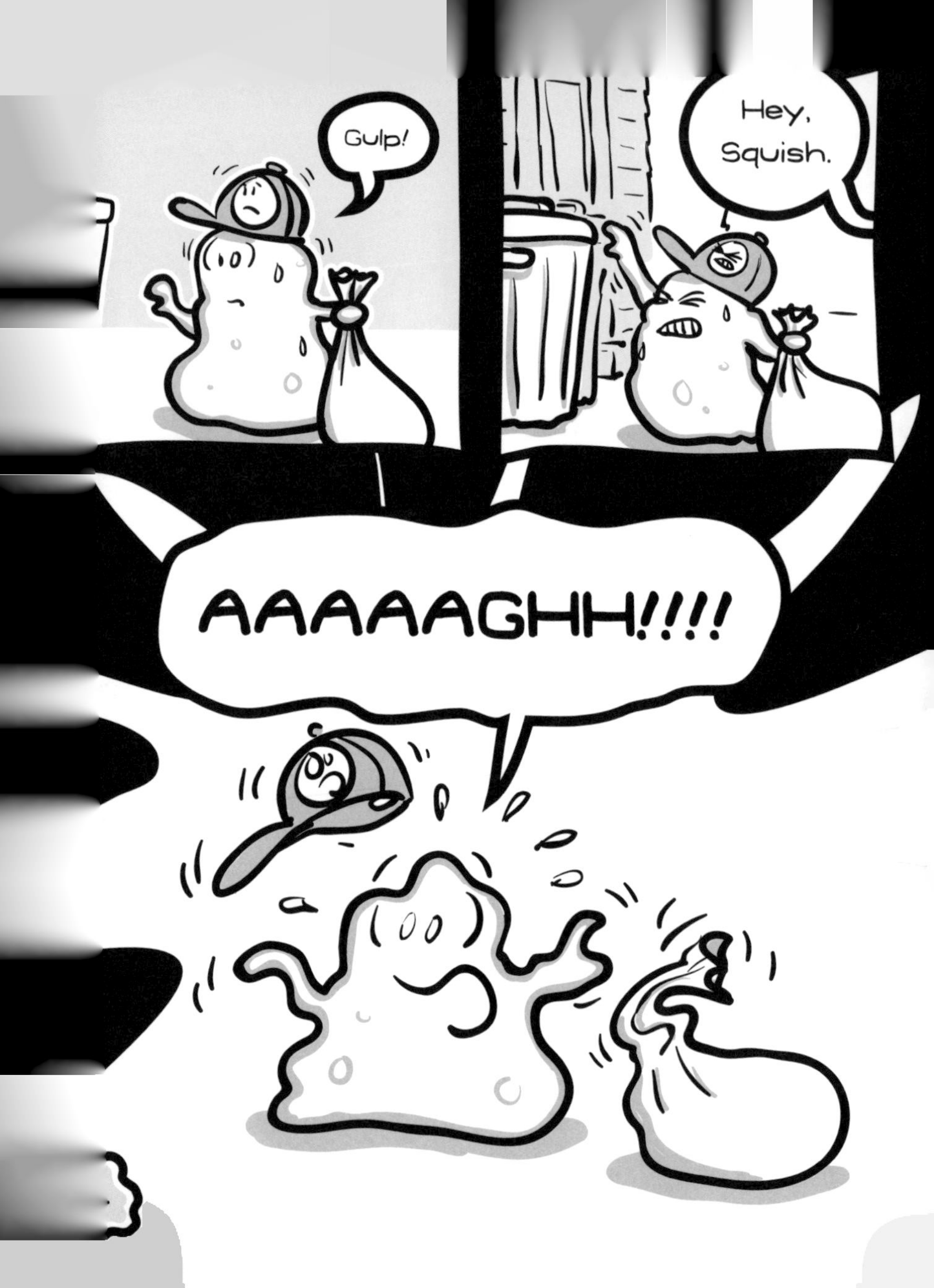
Gulp!
Hey, Squish.
AAAAAGHH!!!!

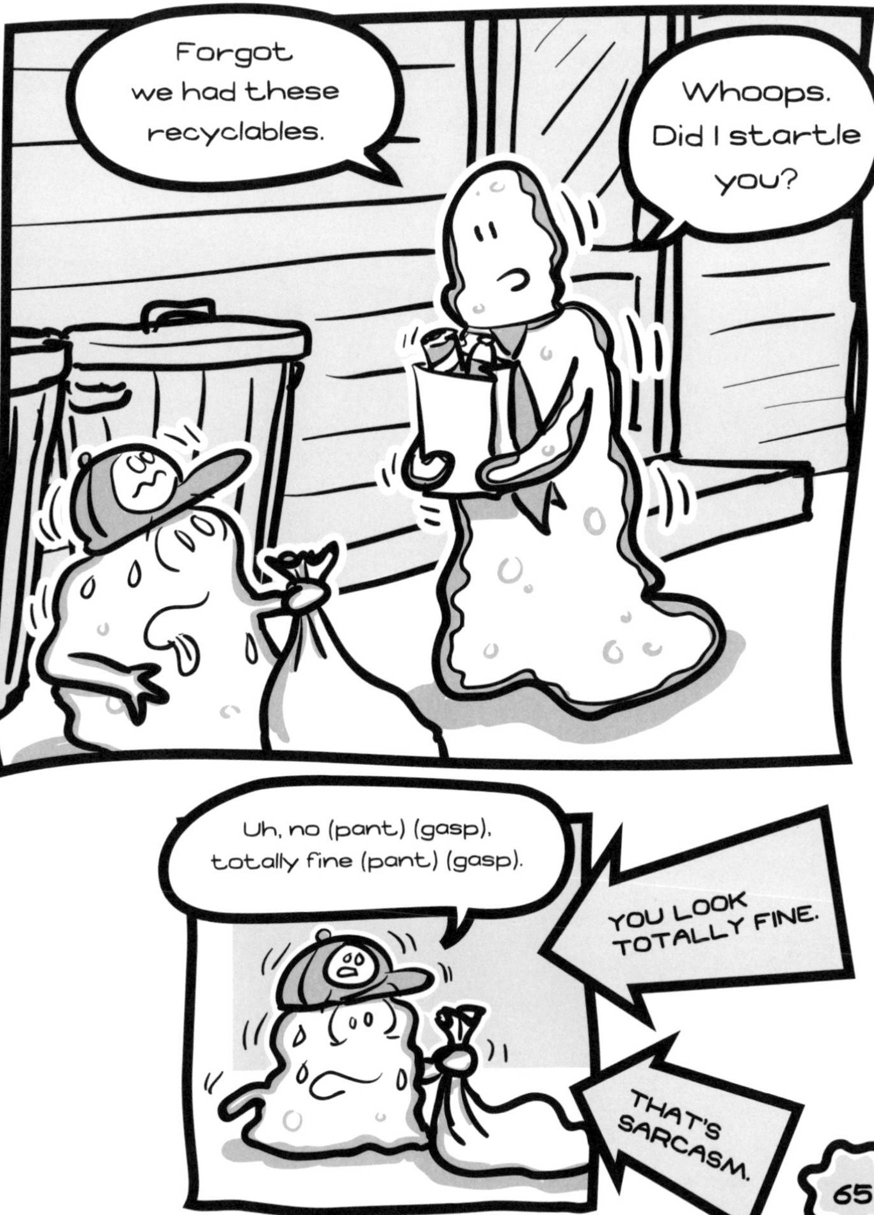
Forgot we had these recyclables.
Whoops. Did I startle you?
Uh, no (pant) (gasp), totally fine (pant) (gasp).
YOU LOOK TOTALLY FINE.
THAT'S SARCASM.

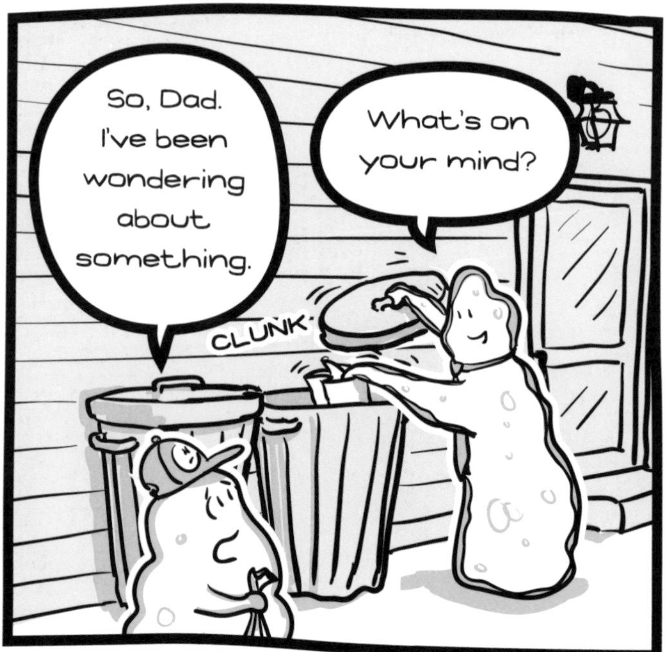
So, Dad. I've been wondering about something.
What's on your mind?
CLUNK

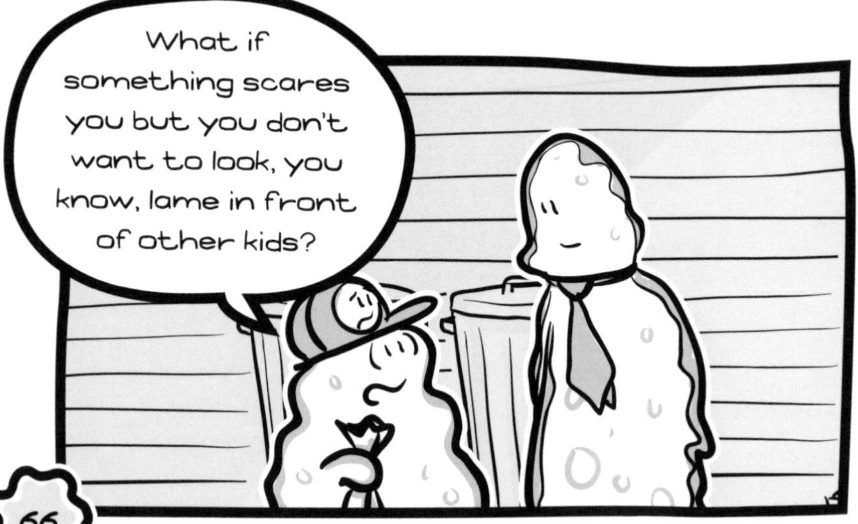
What if something scares you but you don't want to look, you know, lame in front of other kids?

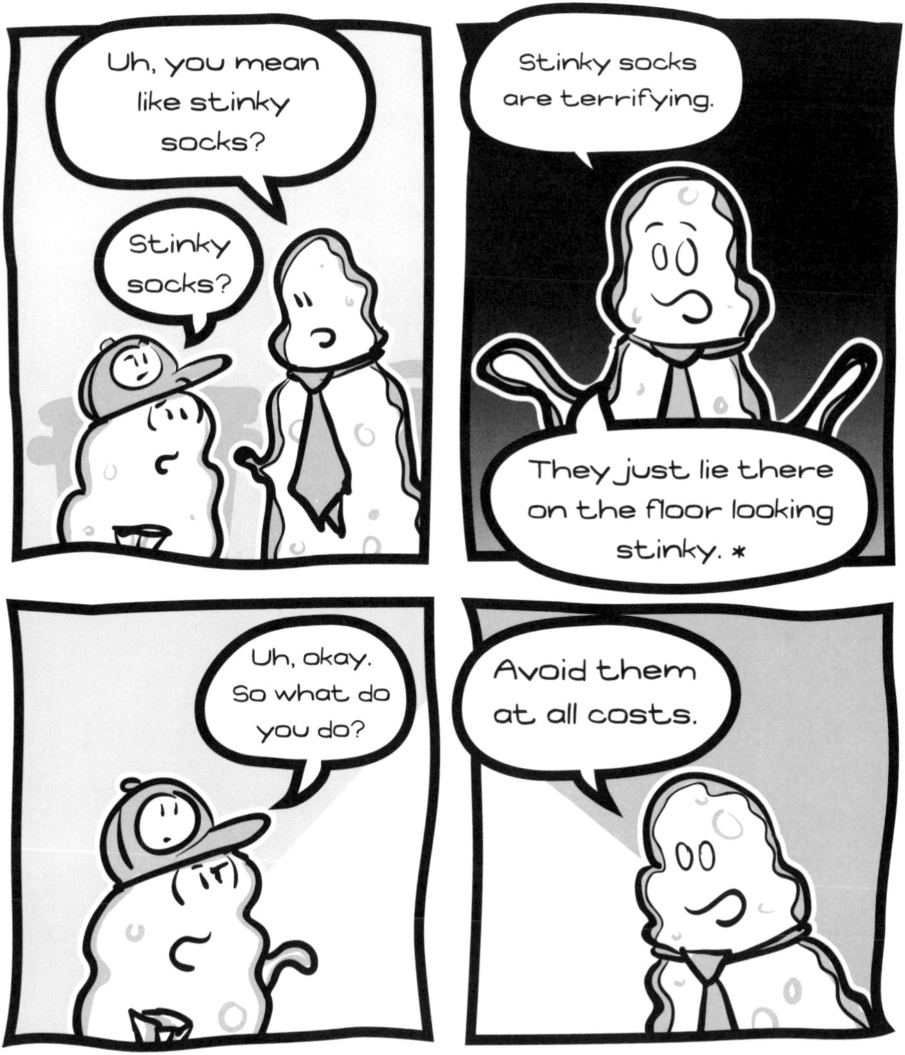
Uh, you mean like stinky socks?
Stinky socks?
Stinky socks are terrifying.
They just lie there on the floor looking stinky. *
Uh, okay. So what do you do?
Avoid them at all costs.

* TRUE SCIENTIFIC FACT: STINKY SOCKS ARE STINKY BECAUSE OF BACTERIA.

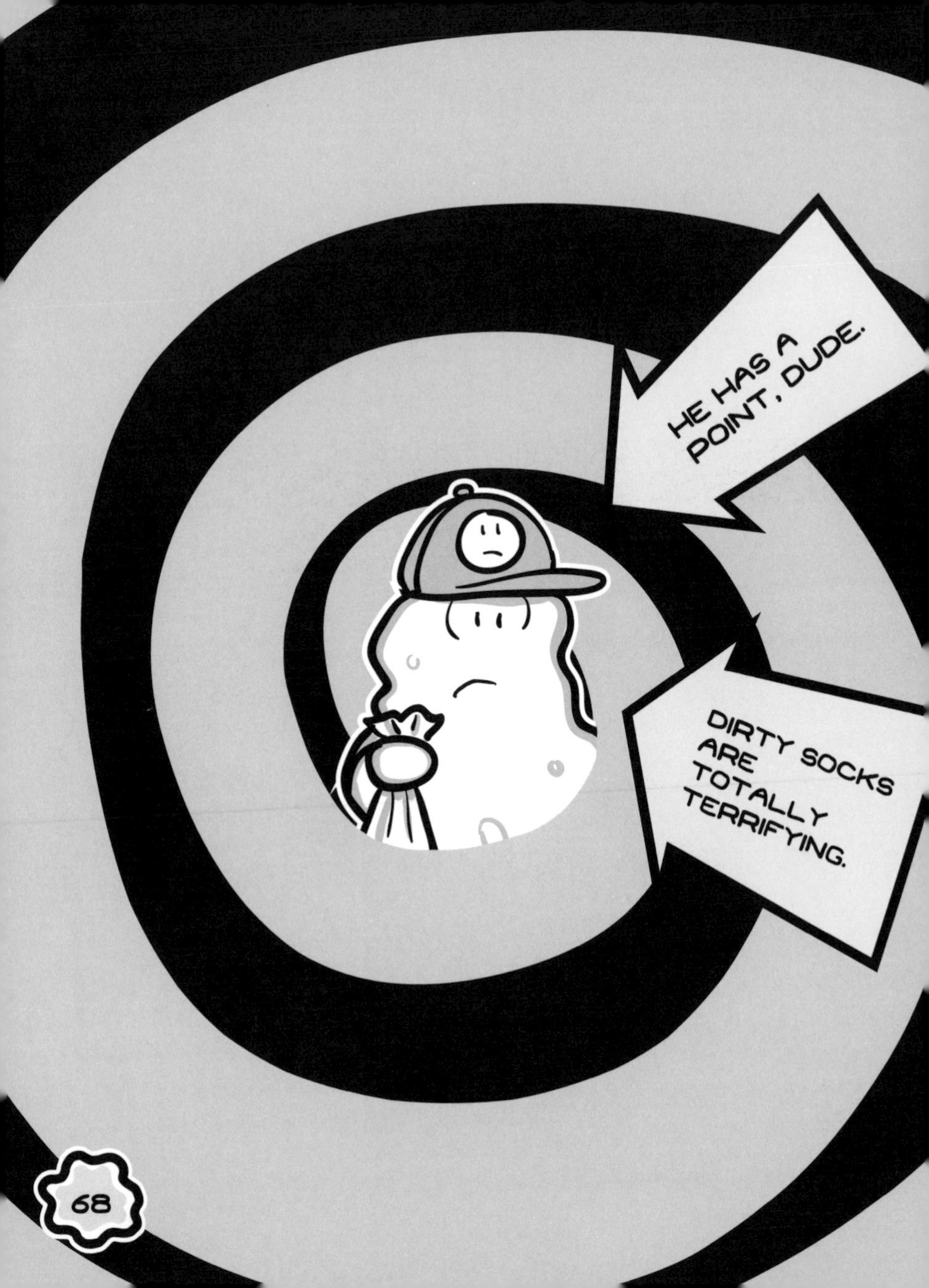
HE HAS A POINT, DUDE.
DIRTY SOCKS ARE TOTALLY TERRIFYING.

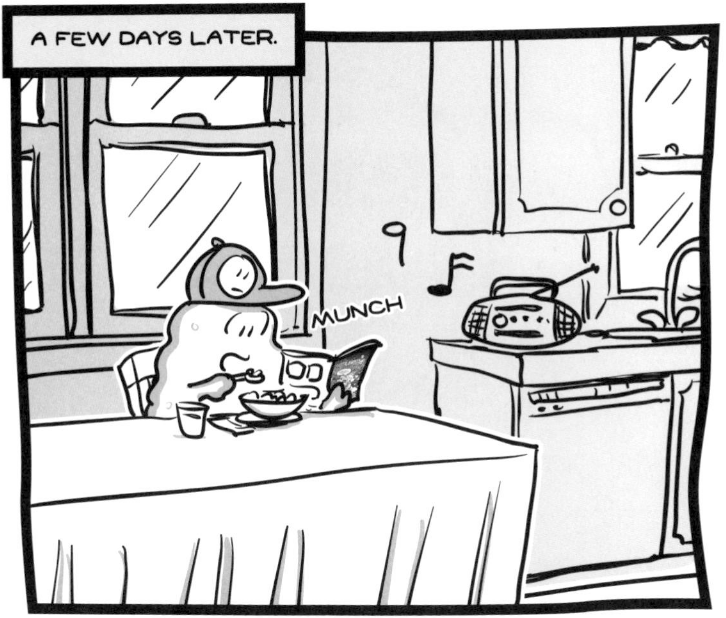
A FEW DAYS LATER.
MUNCH

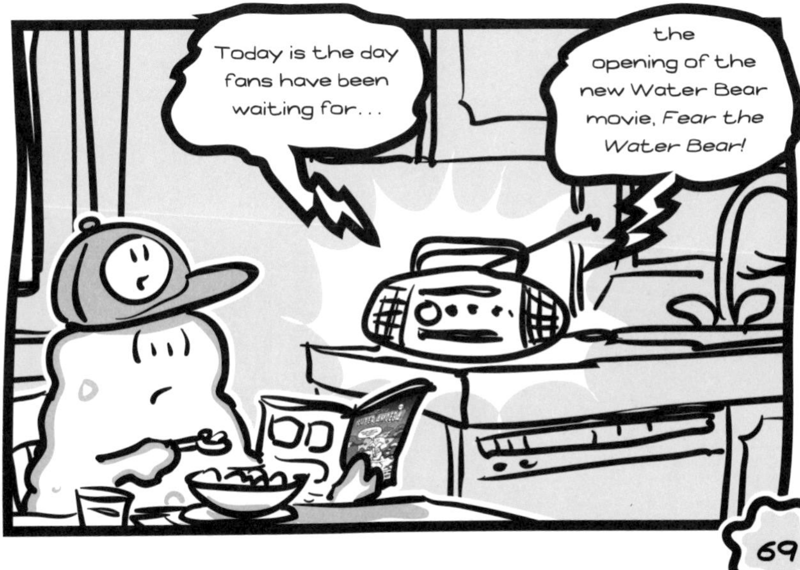
Today is the day fans have been waiting for. . .
the opening of the new Water Bear movie, *Fear the Water Bear!*

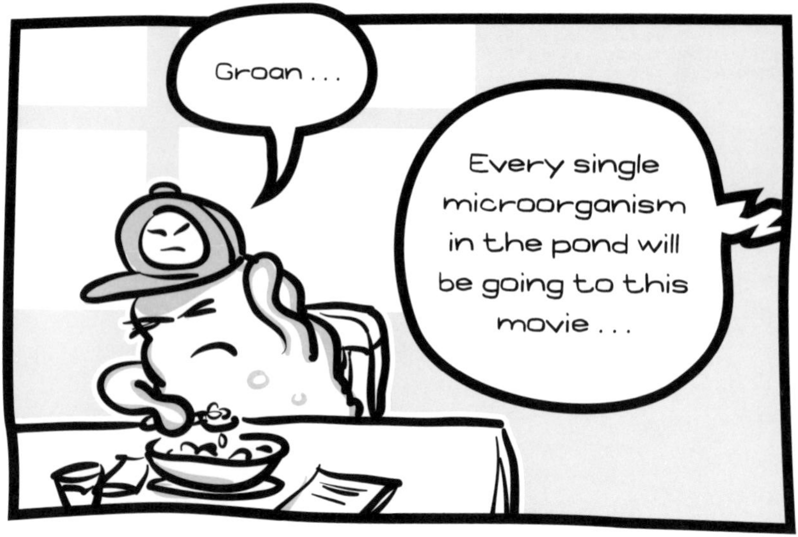
Groan . . .
Every single microorganism in the pond will be going to this movie . . .

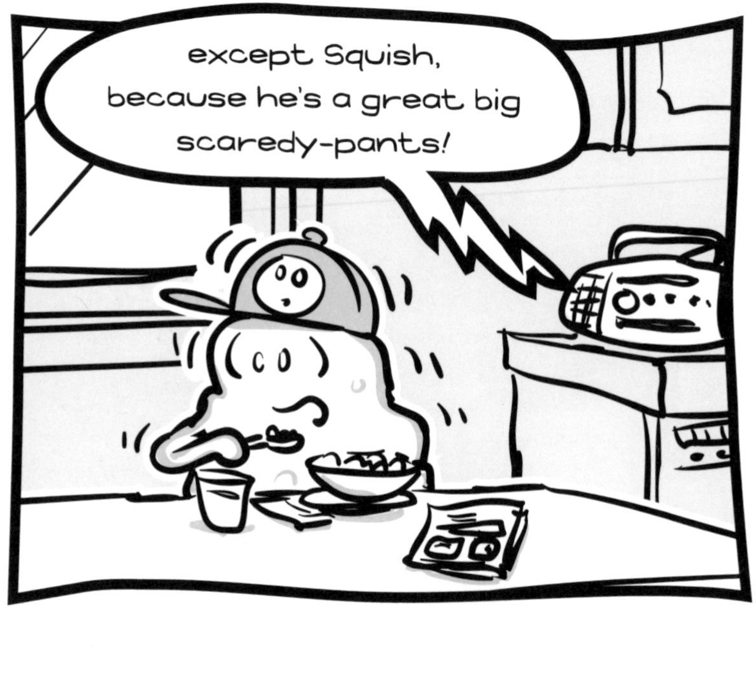
except Squish, because he's a great big scaredy-pants!

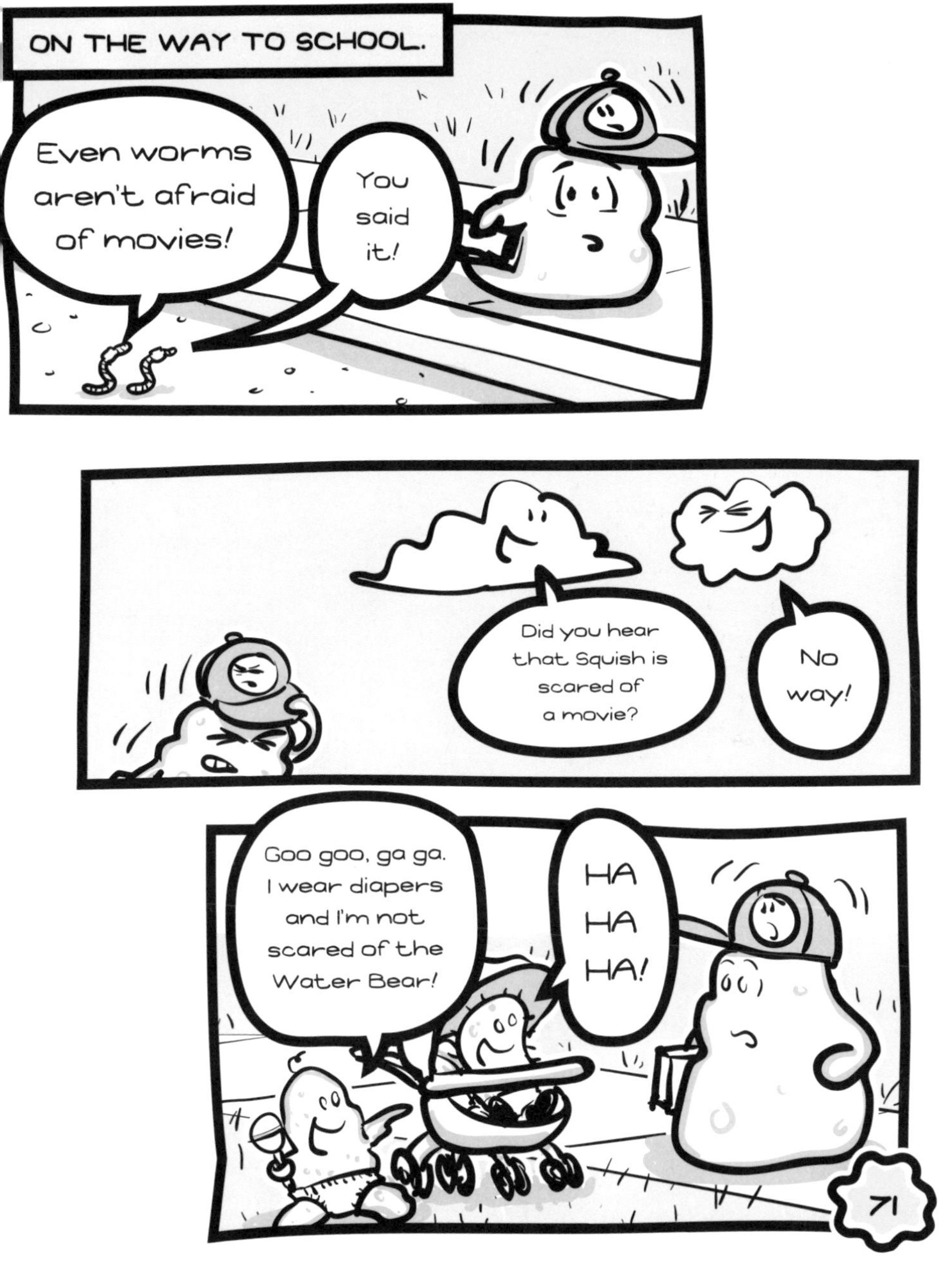
ON THE WAY TO SCHOOL.
Even worms aren't afraid of movies!
You said it!
Did you hear that Squish is scared of a movie?
No way!
Goo goo, ga ga. I wear diapers and I'm not scared of the Water Bear!
HA HA HA!

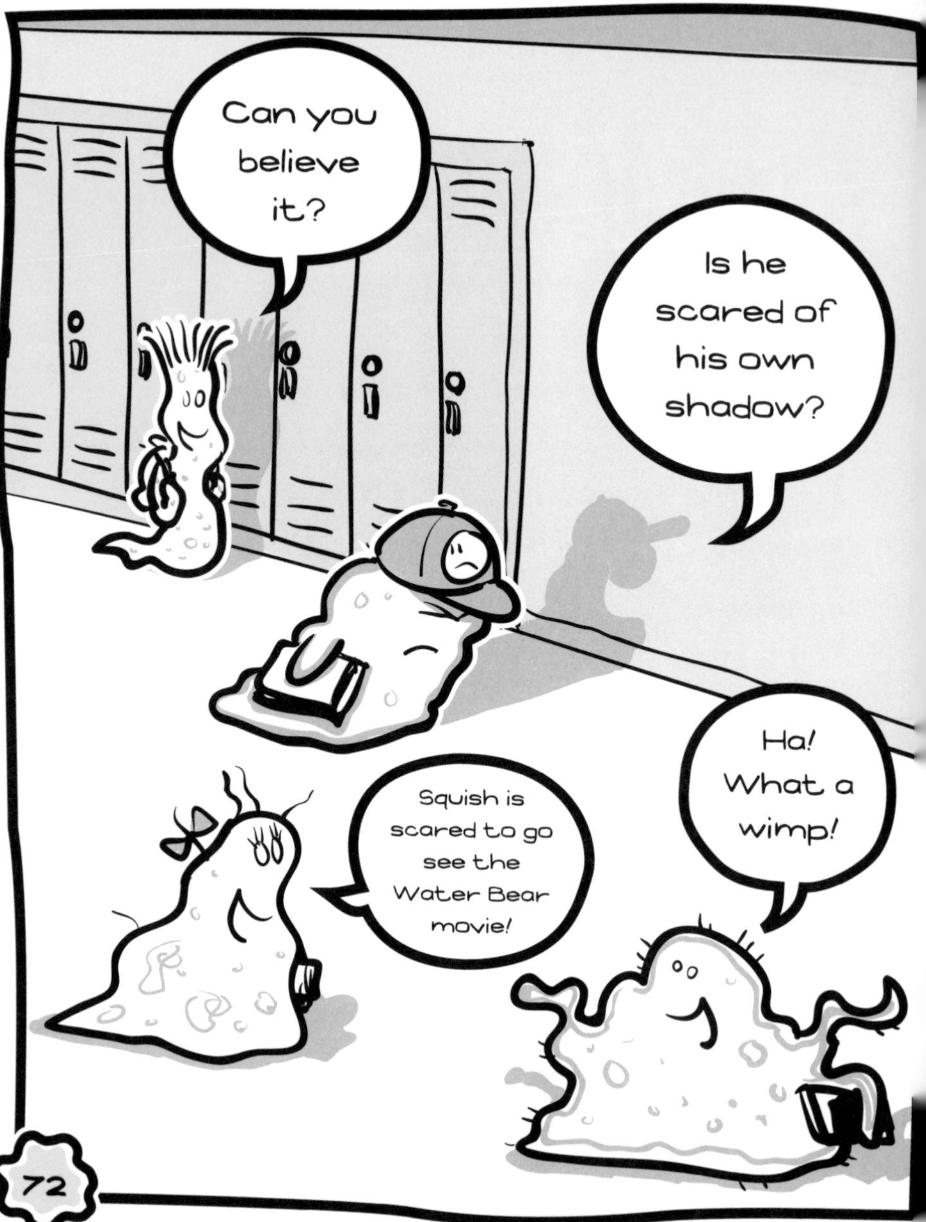
Can you believe it?
Is he scared of his own shadow?
Squish is scared to go see the Water Bear movie!
Ha! What a wimp!

ARED OF A MOVIE? I HEARD IT'S TRUE! BU
E WATER BEAR ISN'T REAL! HECK, IT ISN
EN ALL THAT SCARY! ONLY A SCAREDY-BA
ULD BE WORRIED ABOUT SOME DUMB OL
TER BEAR COMING AFTER YOU! HA HA H
HA! DID YOU HEAR THAT SQUISH IS AFRAID
HE MUST BE A BABY. NO WAY! EVEN BABI
EN'T SCARED OF MOVIES LIKE THAT. WH
LITTLE SISTER SAW THE WATER BEA
VIE AND SHE WASN'T SCARED AT ALL. DO
STILL TAKE NAPS? HA HA HA! I WONDE
HE'S SCARED OF KITTENS AND RAINBOW
ET HE IS! SCAREDY-CAT. HE'S PROBABL
CH A SCAREDY-CAT THAT HE'S SCARE
CATS, TOO! HOW CAN HE BE SO TOTALL
ME? LAME. SO, SO LAME. WHAT A BABY.
SCARED OF FLOWERS? SCAREDY-CAT! HE
RED! WHAT A ... SCARED OF A MOV
SCAREDY SCA... ISH-SQUISH! HA H
HA HA! SAD PA... MP. HOW OLD IS H
WAY? HE MU... E IN KINDERGARTE
IT'S NOT EVE... MY BABY BRO...R
NDERGARTEN, AND HE ISN'T SCARED ... AN

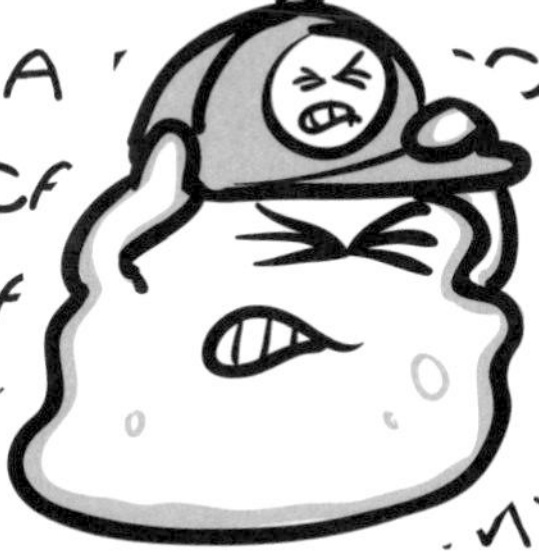

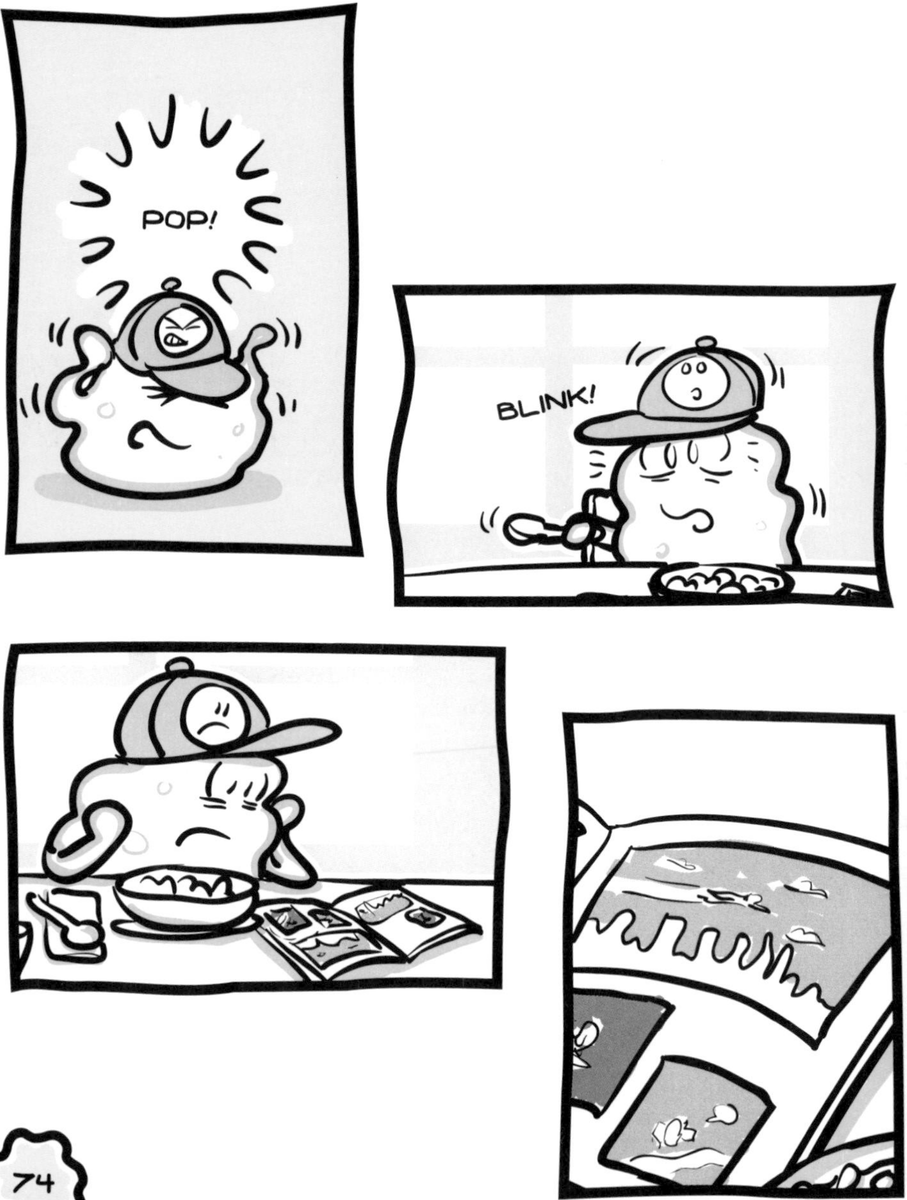
POP!
BLINK!

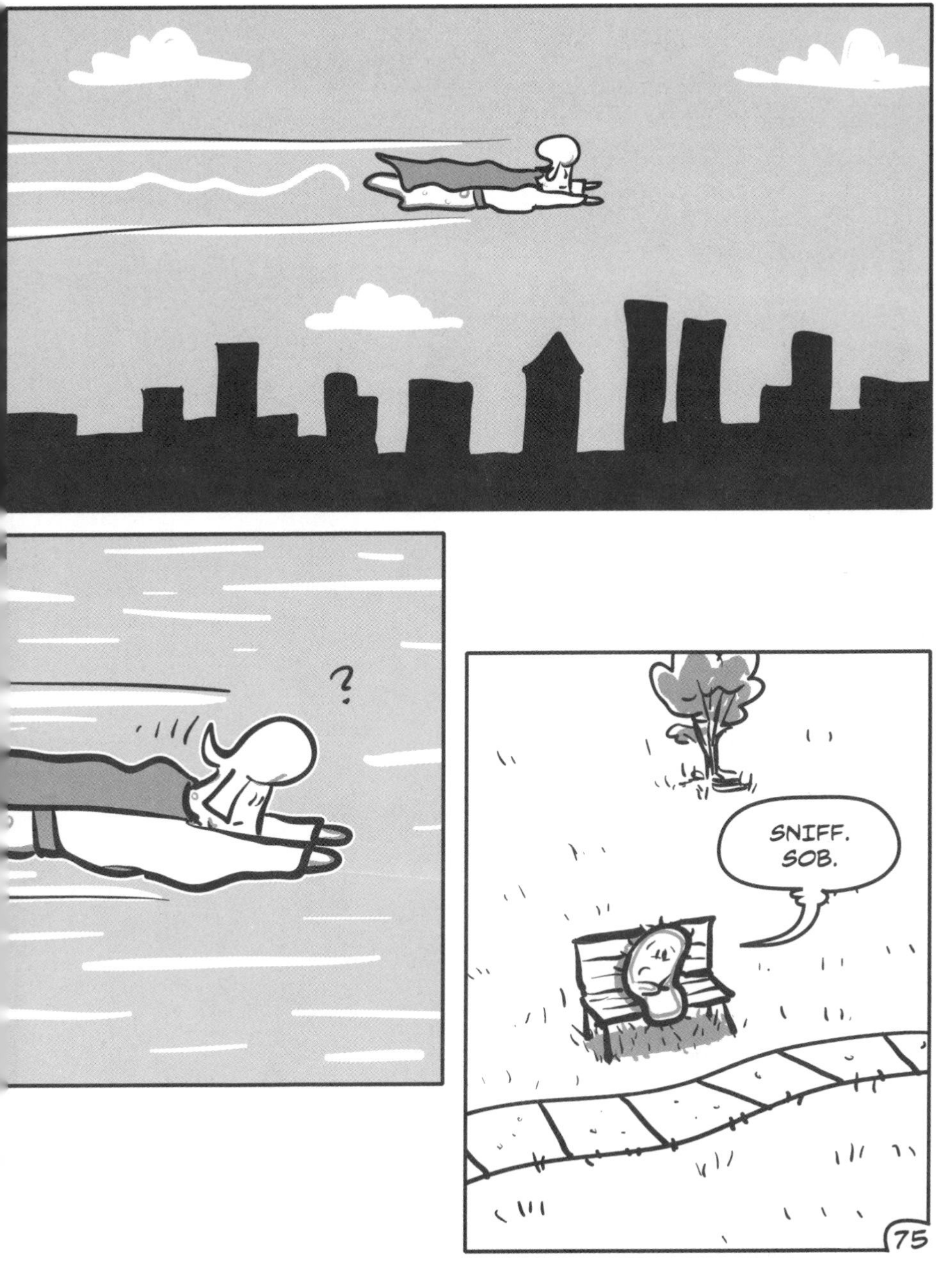
?
SNIFF. SOB.

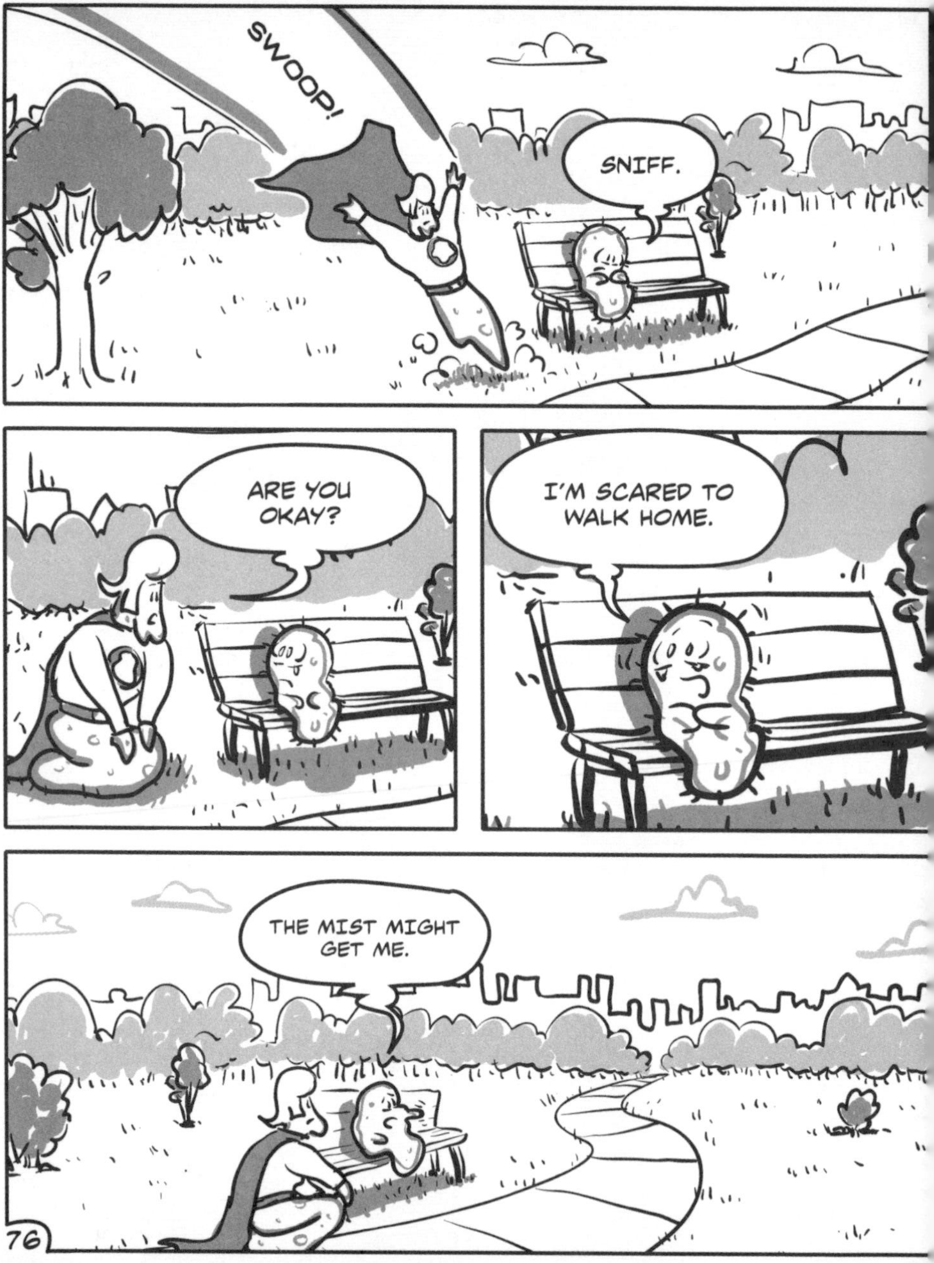
SWOOP!
SNIFF.
ARE YOU OKAY?
I'M SCARED TO WALK HOME.
THE MIST MIGHT GET ME.

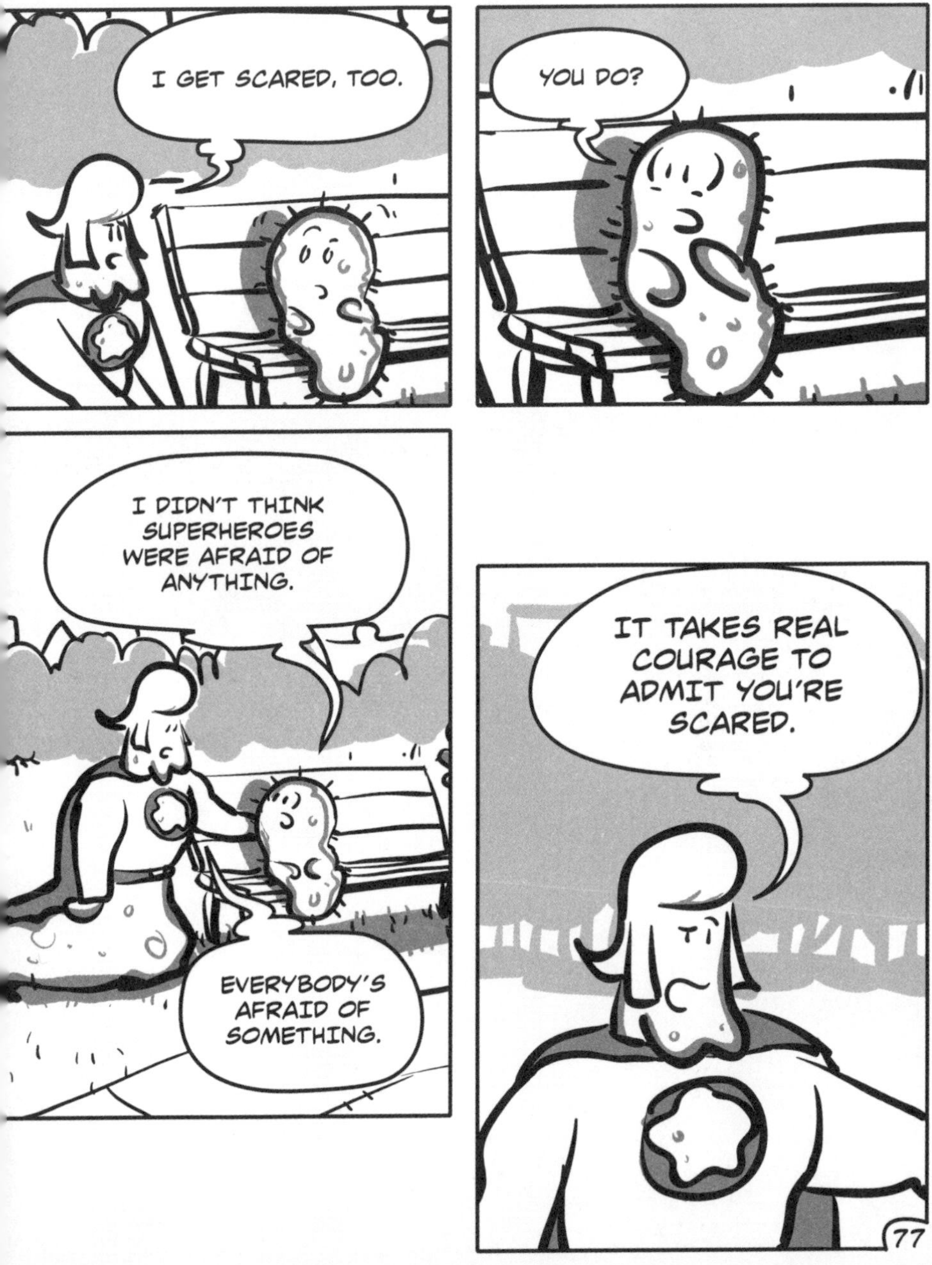

I GET SCARED, TOO.
YOU DO?
I DIDN'T THINK SUPERHEROES WERE AFRAID OF ANYTHING.
EVERYBODY'S AFRAID OF SOMETHING.
IT TAKES REAL COURAGE TO ADMIT YOU'RE SCARED.

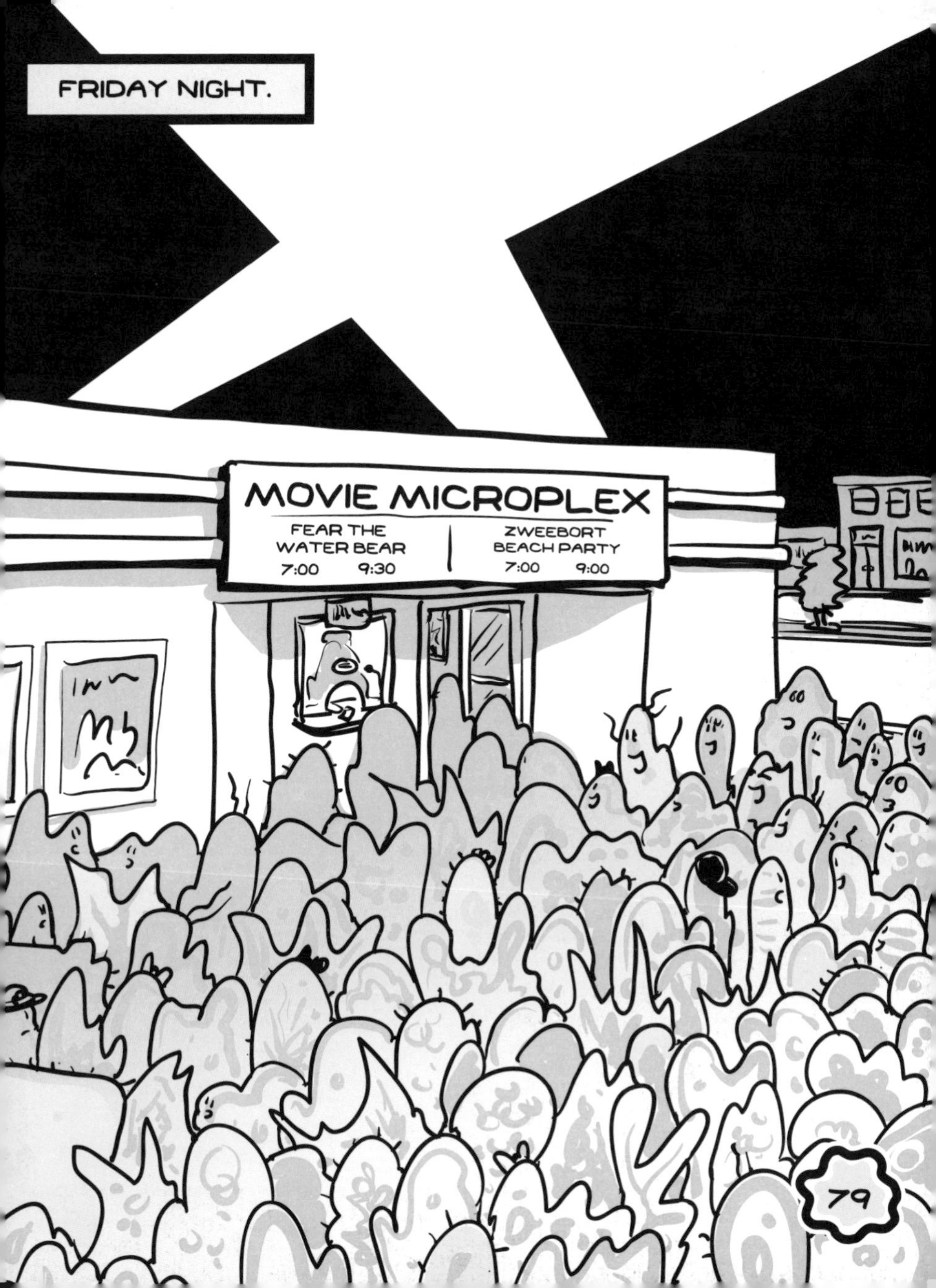
FRIDAY NIGHT.
MOVIE MICROPLEX
FEAR THE WATER BEAR
7:00 9:30
ZWEEBORT BEACH PARTY
7:00 9:00

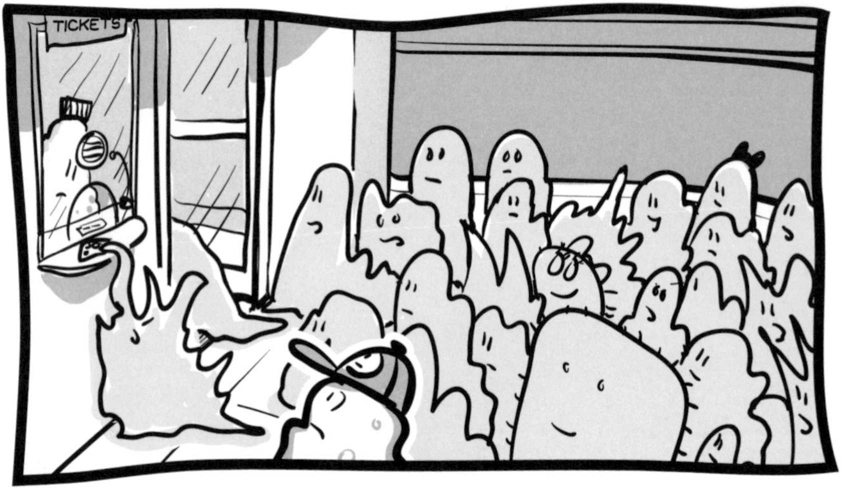
TICKETS

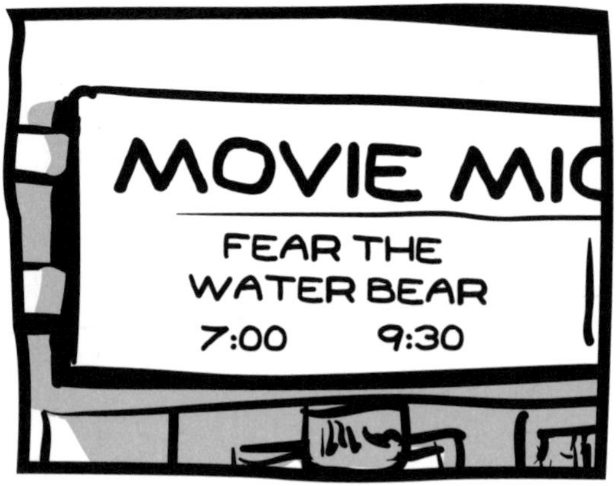
MOVIE MIC
FEAR THE
WATER BEAR
7:00 9:30

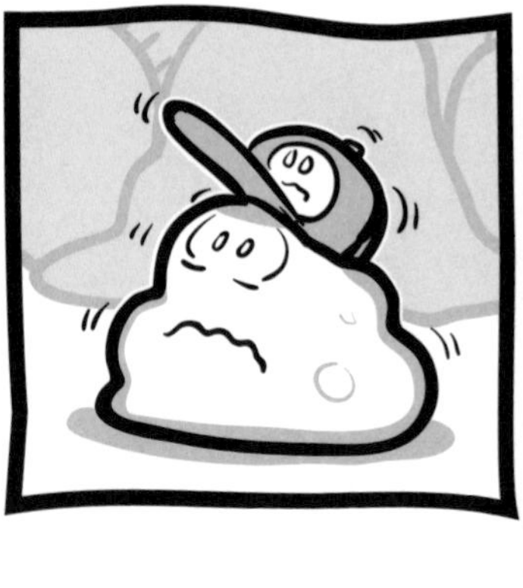

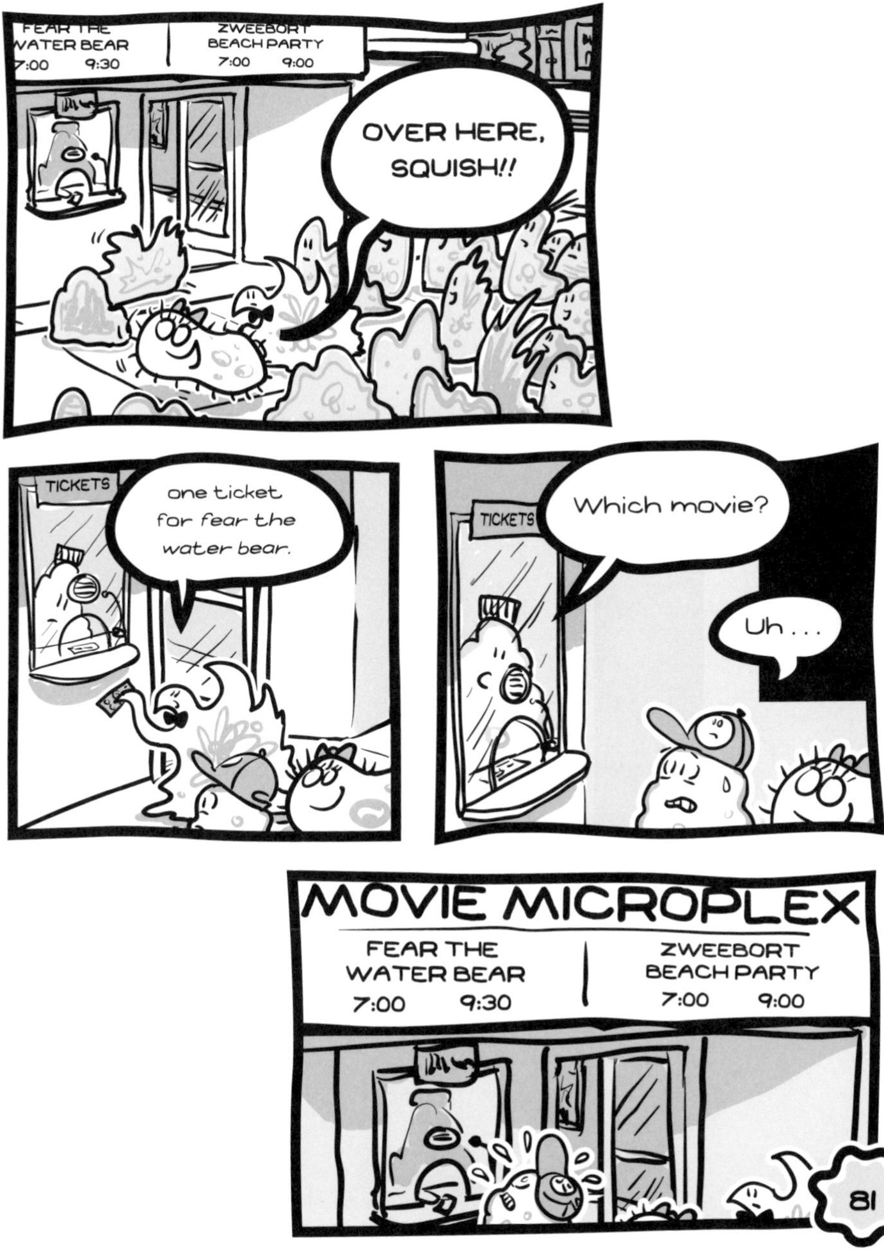
ZWEEBORT BEACH PARTY 7:00 9:00
OVER HERE, SQUISH!!
TICKETS
one ticket for *fear the water bear.*
TICKETS
Which movie?
Uh . . .
MOVIE MICROPLEX
FEAR THE WATER BEAR 7:00 9:30
ZWEEBORT BEACH PARTY 7:00 9:00

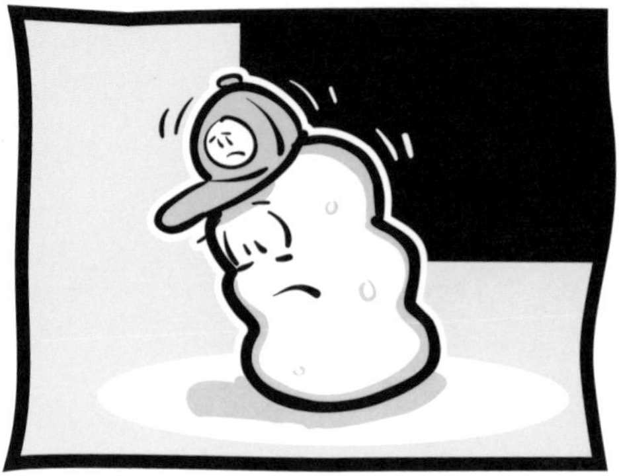

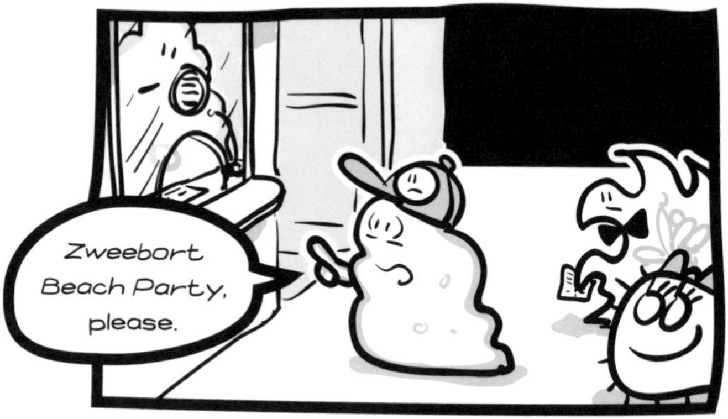
Zweebort Beach Party, please.

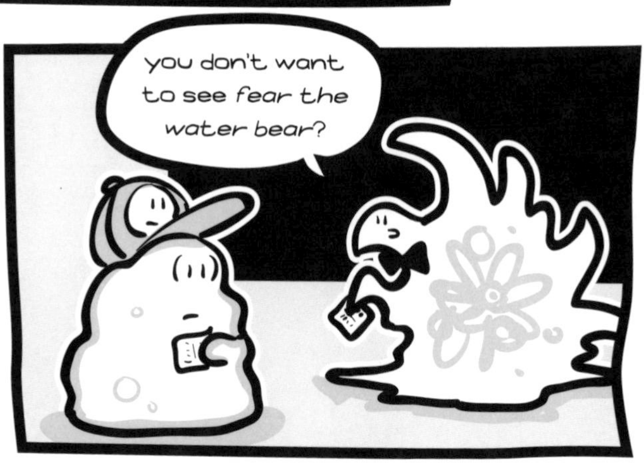
you don't want to see fear the water bear?

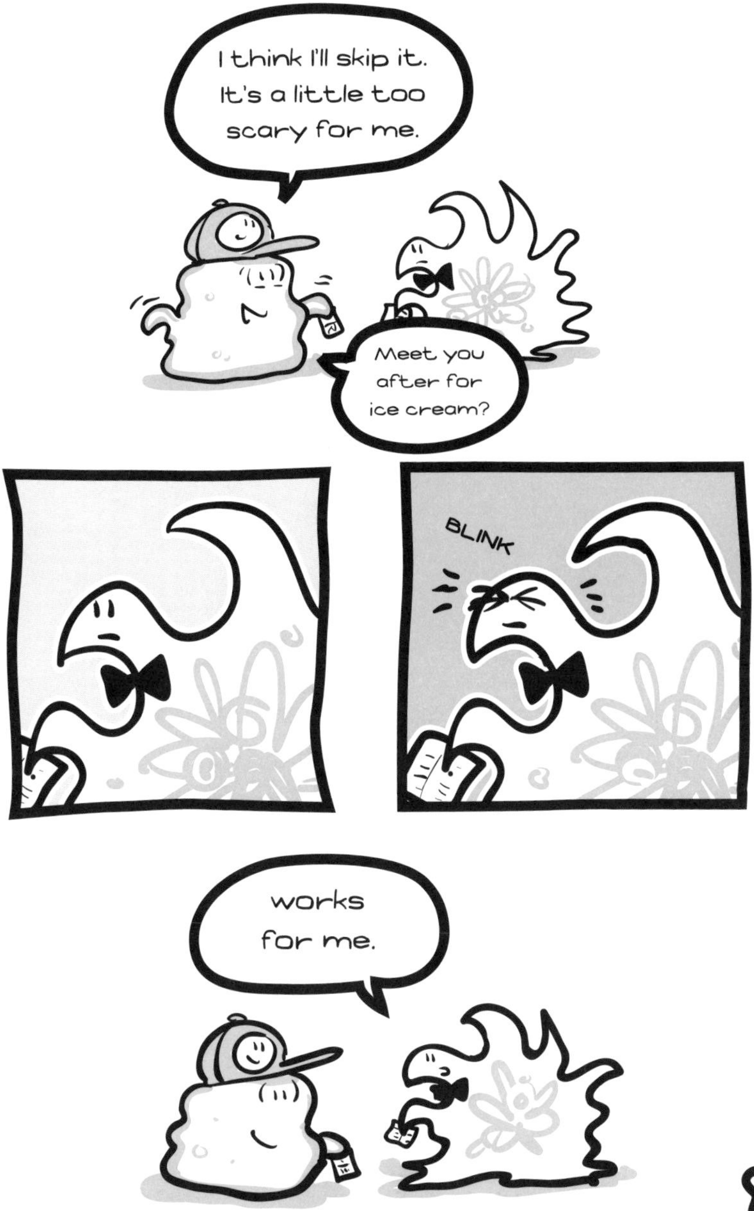
I think I'll skip it. It's a little too scary for me.
Meet you after for ice cream?
BLINK
works for me.

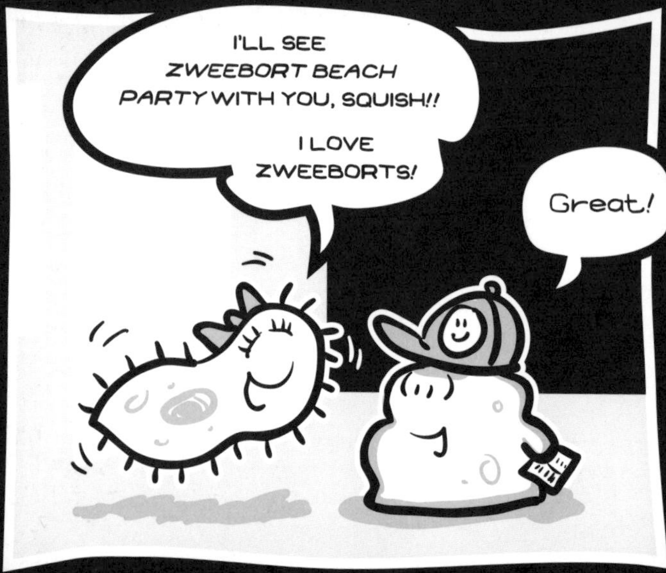
I'LL SEE *ZWEEBORT BEACH PARTY* WITH YOU, SQUISH!!
I LOVE ZWEEBORTS!
Great!

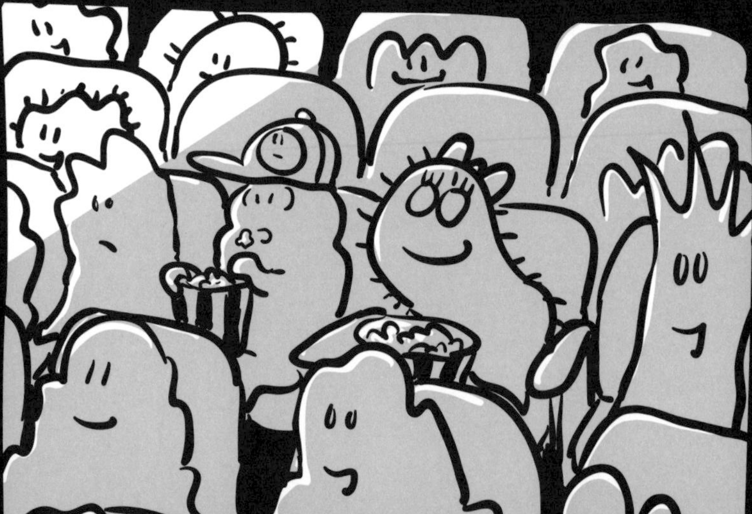

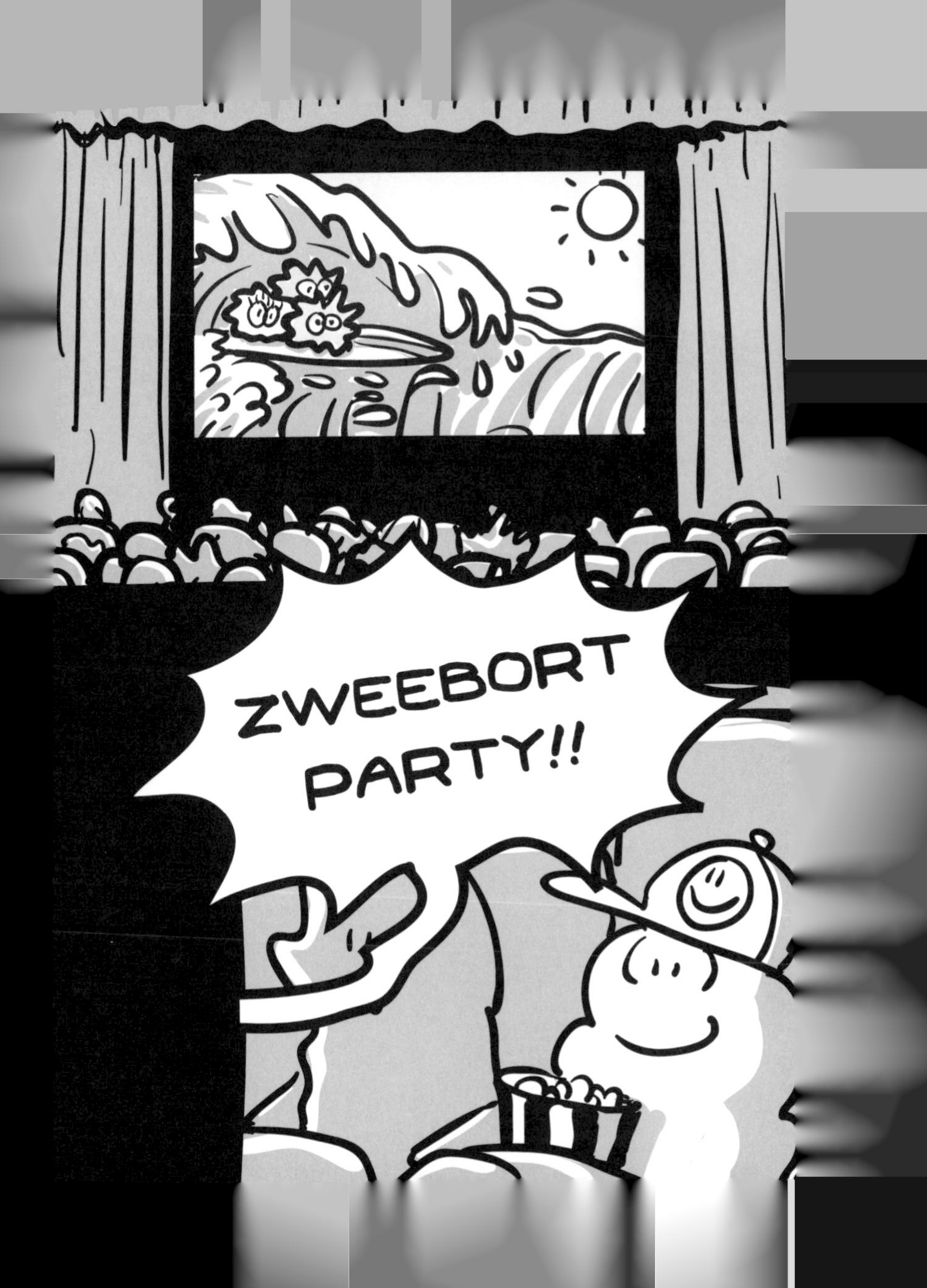
ZWEEBORT PARTY!!

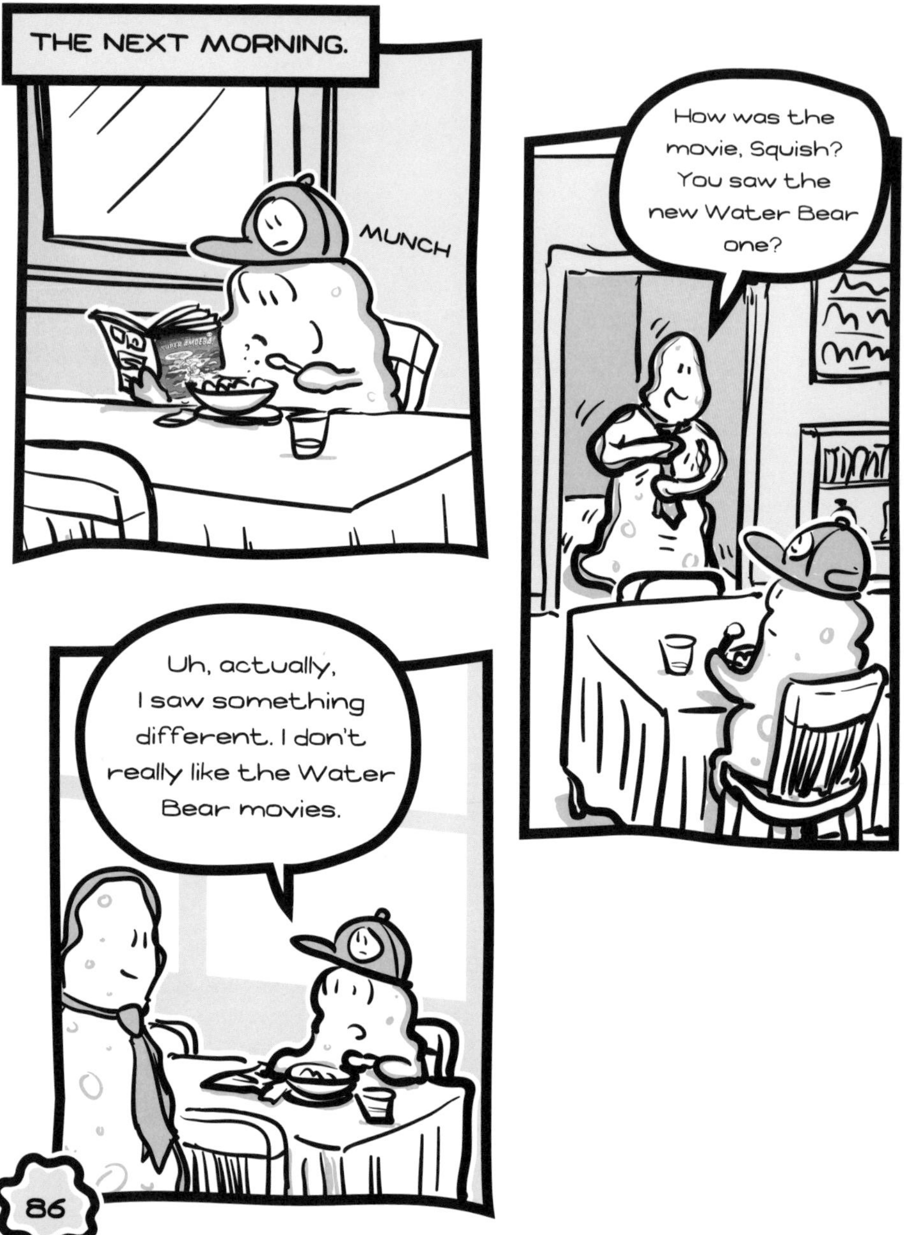
THE NEXT MORNING.
MUNCH
How was the movie, Squish? You saw the new Water Bear one?
Uh, actually, I saw something different. I don't really like the Water Bear movies.

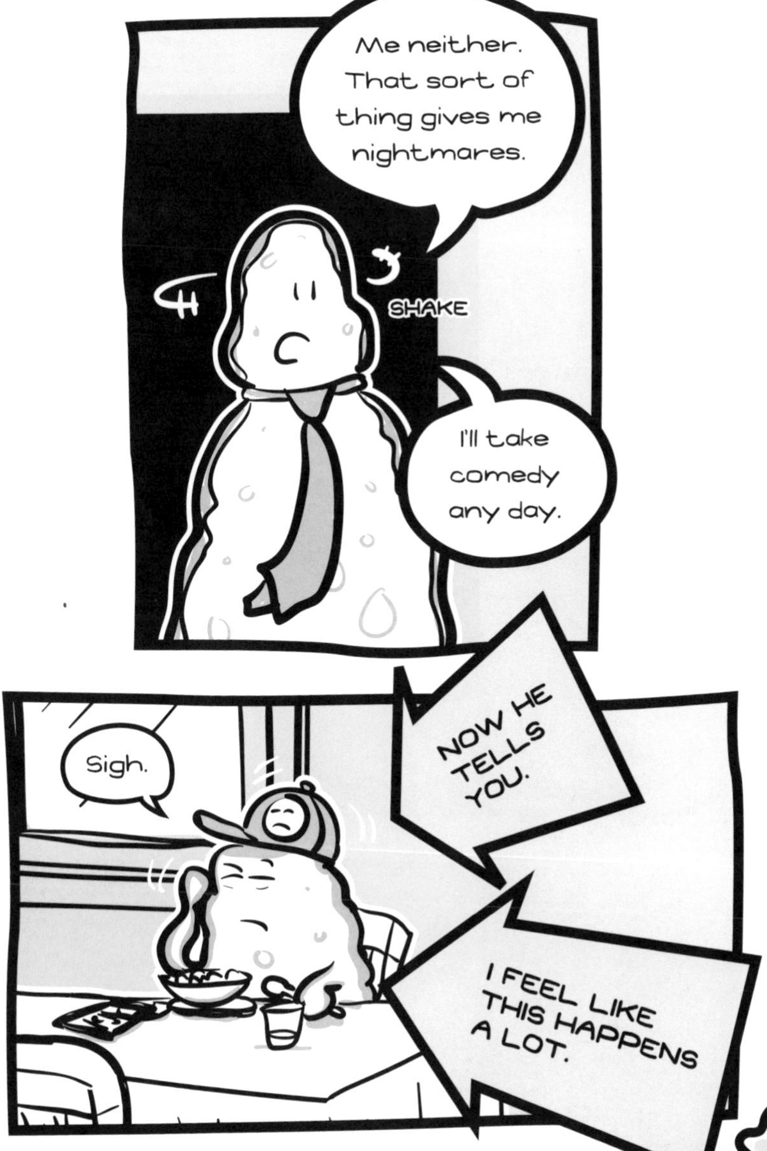

Me neither. That sort of thing gives me nightmares.
SHAKE
I'll take comedy any day.
Sigh.
NOW HE TELLS YOU.
I FEEL LIKE THIS HAPPENS A LOT.

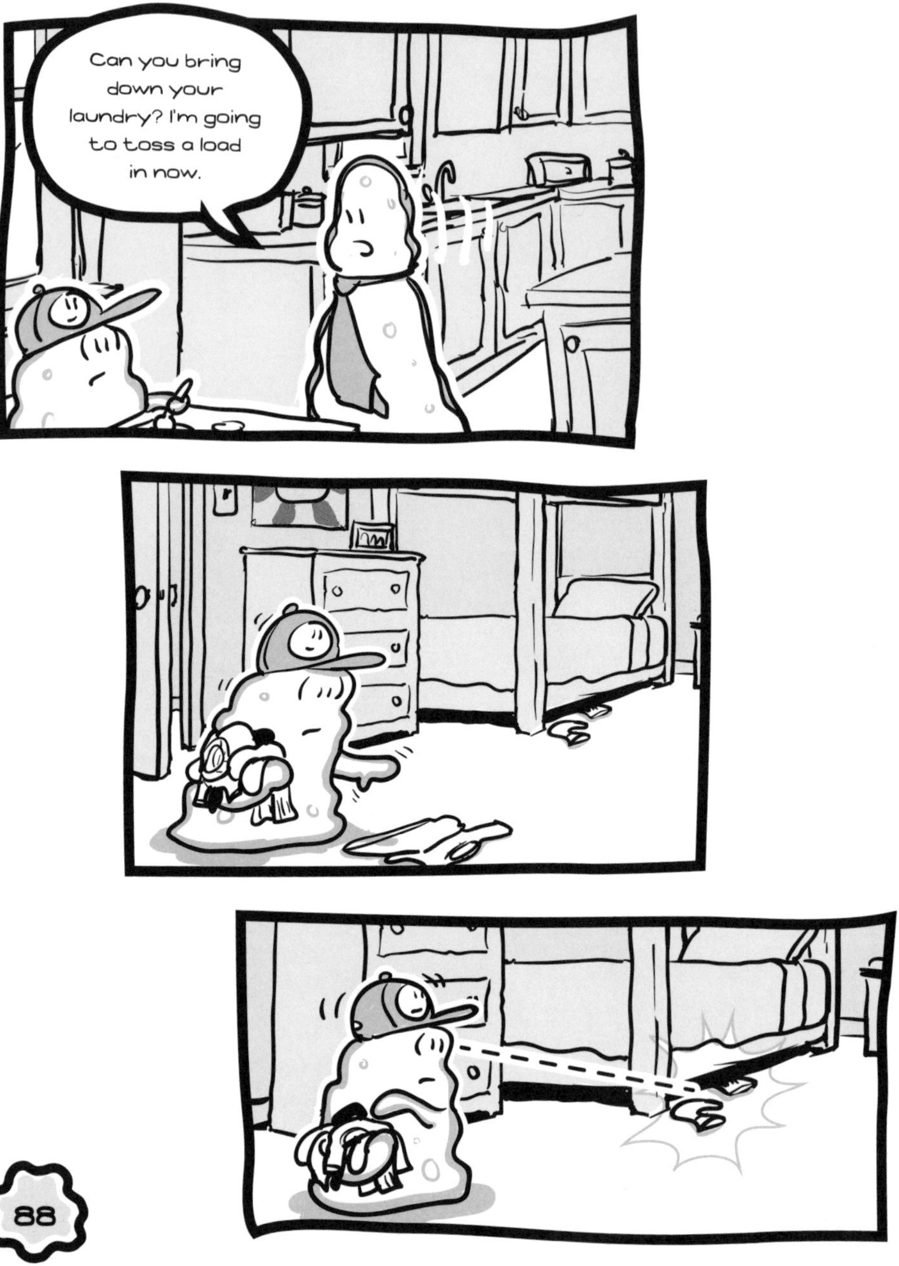
Can you bring down your laundry? I'm going to toss a load in now.

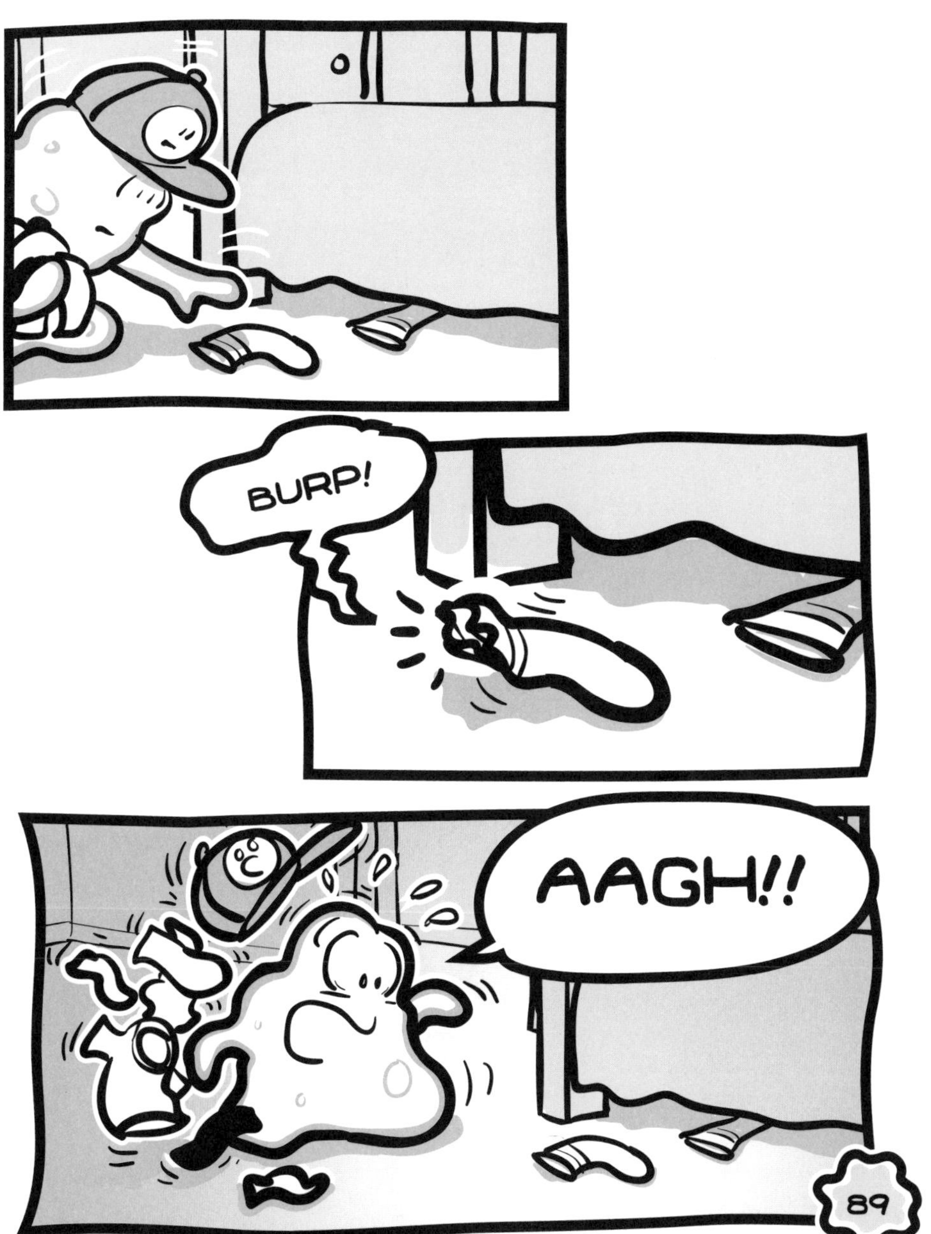
BURP!
AAGH!!

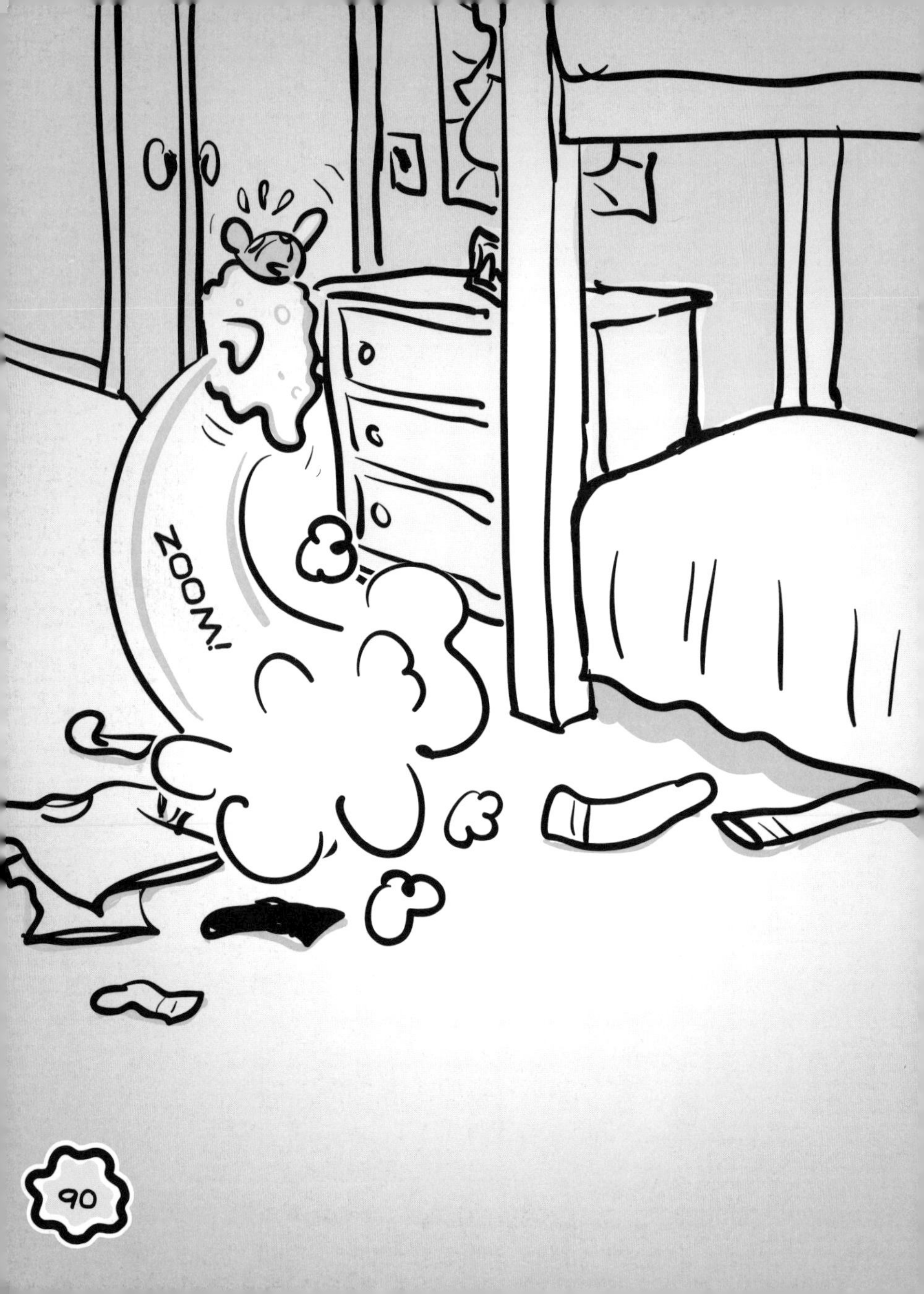
ZOOM!

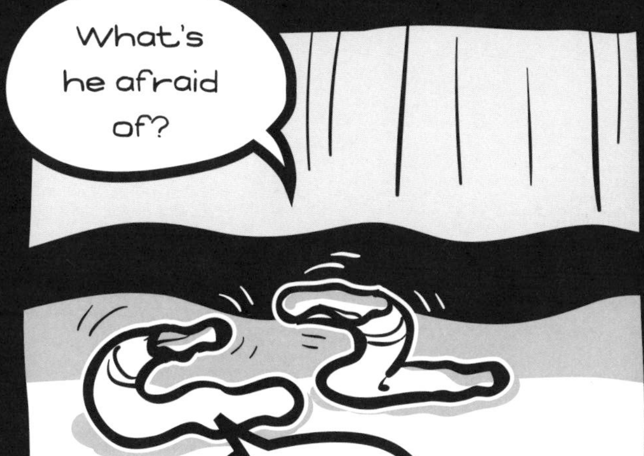
What's he afraid of?
Got me.

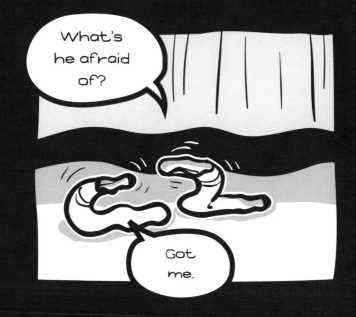

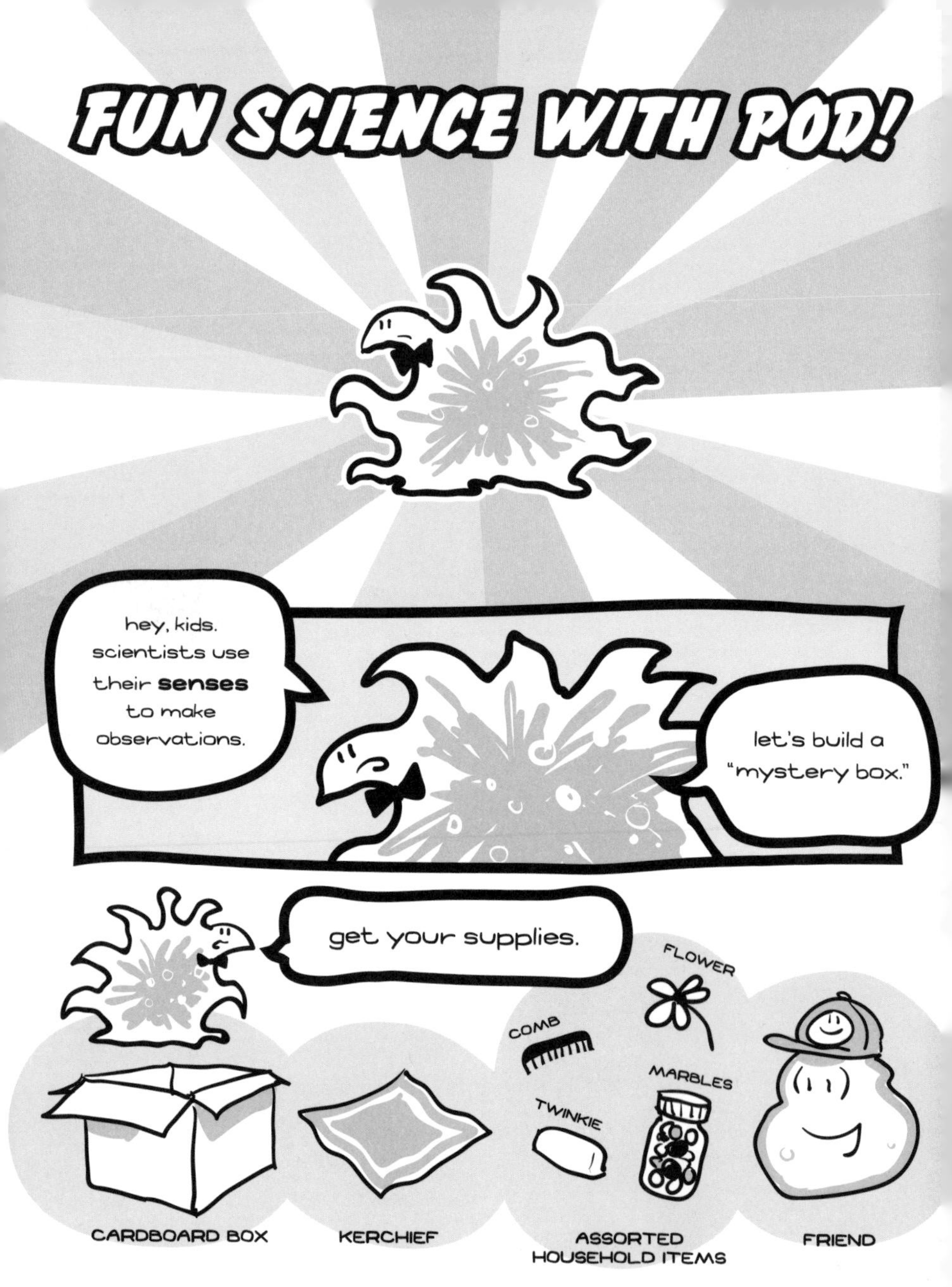
FUN SCIENCE WITH POD!
hey, kids. scientists use their **senses** to make observations.
let's build a "mystery box."
get your supplies.
CARDBOARD BOX
KERCHIEF
COMB
FLOWER
TWINKIE
MARBLES
ASSORTED HOUSEHOLD ITEMS
FRIEND

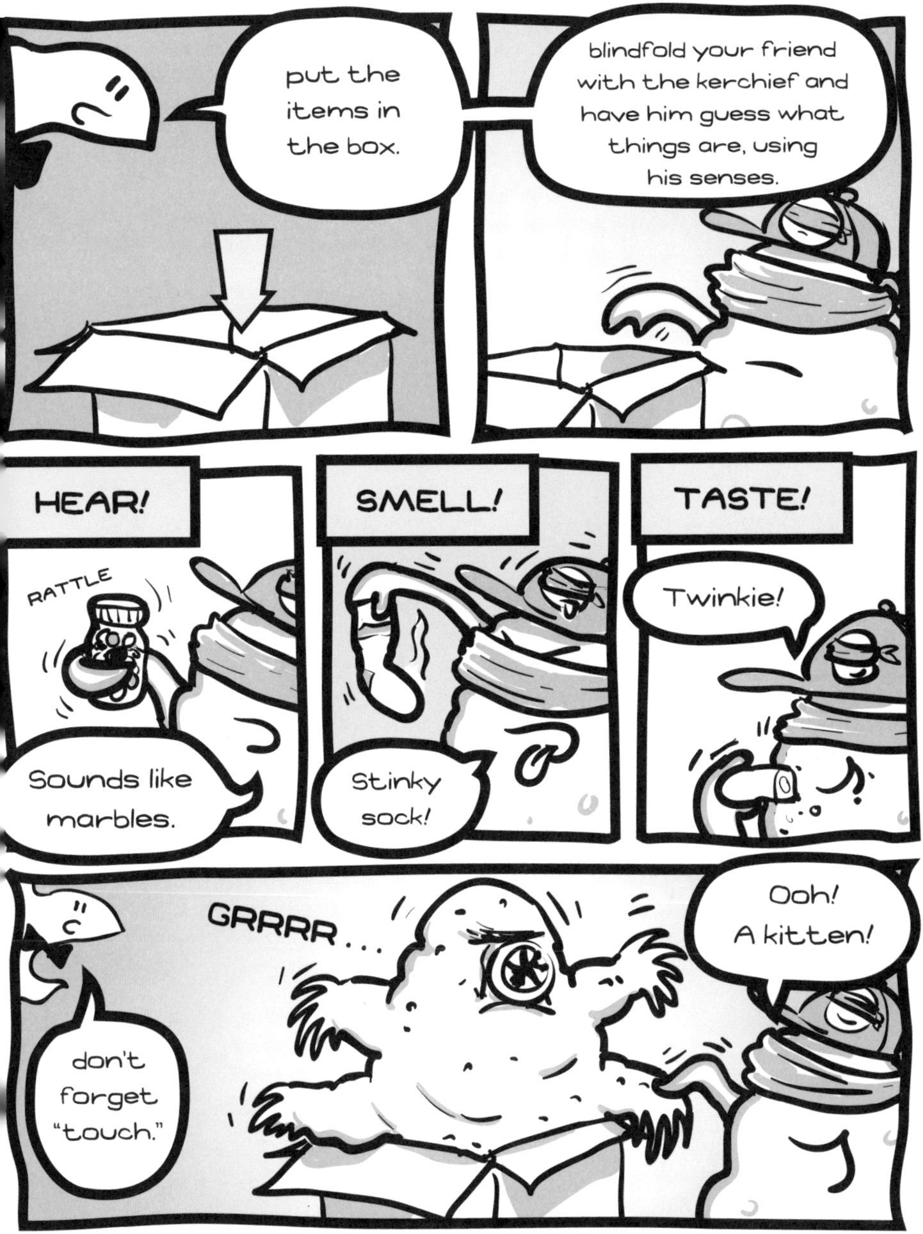
put the items in the box.
blindfold your friend with the kerchief and have him guess what things are, using his senses.
HEAR!
RATTLE
Sounds like marbles.
SMELL!
Stinky sock!
TASTE!
Twinkie!
GRRRR. . . .
Ooh! A kitten!
don't forget "touch."

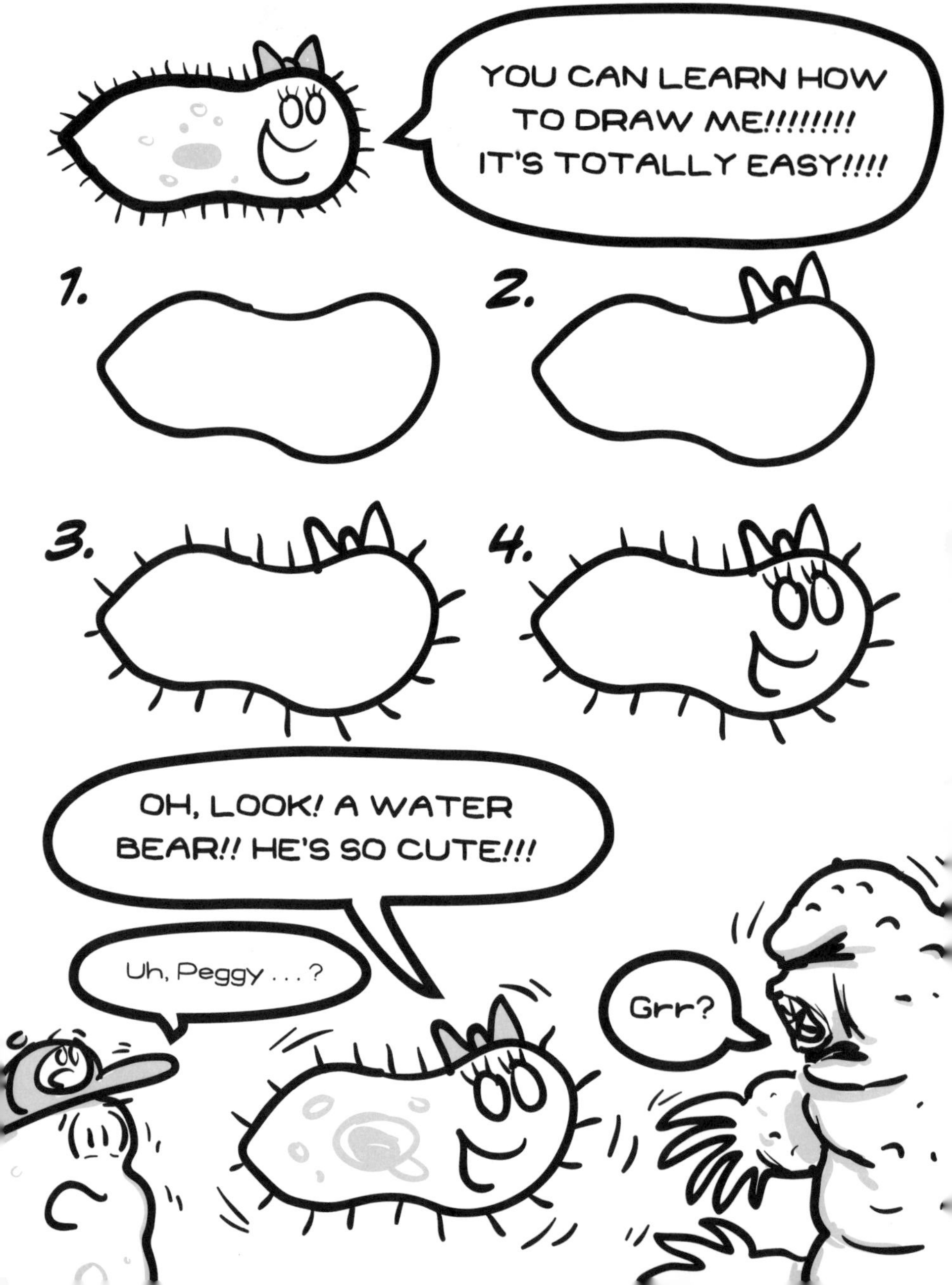
YOU CAN LEARN HOW TO DRAW ME!!!!!!!!! IT'S TOTALLY EASY!!!!
1.
2.
3.
4.
OH, LOOK! A WATER BEAR!! HE'S SO CUTE!!!
Uh, Peggy . . . ?
Grr?

IF YOU LIKE SQUISH, YOU'LL LOVE BABYMOUSE!

#1 BABYMOUSE: Queen of the World!

#2 BABYMOUSE: Our Hero

#3 BABYMOUSE: Beach Babe

#4 BABYMOUSE: Rock Star

#5 BABYMOUSE: Heartbreaker

#6 CAMP BABYMOUSE

#7 BABYMOUSE: Skater Girl

#8 BABYMOUSE: Puppy Love

#9 BABYMOUSE: Monster Mash

#10 BABYMOUSE: The Musical

#11 BABYMOUSE: Dragonslayer

#12 BABYMOUSE: Burns Rubber

#13 BABYMOUSE: Cupcake Tycoon

#14 BABYMOUSE: Mad Scientist

#15 A Very BABYMOUSE Christmas

#16 BABYMOUSE for President

#17 Extreme BABYMOUSE

#18 Happy Birthday, BABYMOUSE

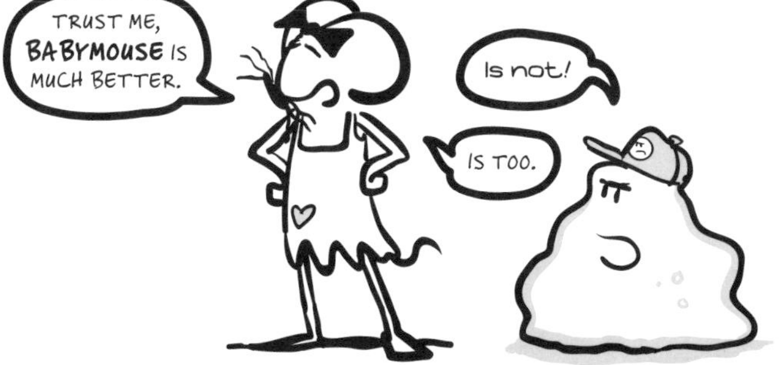
TRUST ME, BABYMOUSE IS MUCH BETTER.
Is not!
IS TOO.

Look for these other great books
by Jennifer L. Holm!

THE BOSTON JANE TRILOGY
EIGHTH GRADE IS MAKING ME SICK
MIDDLE SCHOOL IS WORSE THAN MEATLOAF
OUR ONLY MAY AMELIA
PENNY FROM HEAVEN
TURTLE IN PARADISE

THEY'RE
REALLY GOOD!
TRUST ME!